All characters in this book are fictitious. Any resemblance to actual people, living or dead, is entirely coincidental. The names, incidents, dialogue and opinions expressed within are products of the author's imagination and are not meant to be construed as real. Nothing is intended or should be interpreted as expressing, or representing, the views of any institution of higher learning.

First paperback edition December 2024

Cover design by Rod Couser | Cover Photo
ID 5534089 | Cowboy Silhouette © Outdoorsman | Dreamstime.com

ISBN 979-8-9896445-1-3 (Hardcover)
ISBN 979-8-9896445-2-0 (Paperback)
ISBN 979-8-9896445-3-7 (eBook)

Chapter I

Bigfork, Montana, February, 1998

It may have seemed cold, but the term differed in meaning amongst the two thousand brave souls living in Bigfork, Montana. During the winter months, those born there usually started conversations about the cold when the thermometer dipped below ten degrees Fahrenheit. Others thought anything below twenty degrees qualified, while newcomers didn't pick a specific temperature. To them, it was always cold.

Walking down a rugged dirt trail, Winston Bartholomew knew the temperature was around fourteen degrees and considered that damn cold. Parts of the trail were dusted in snow that crunched under the weight of his size fourteen boots, not that it mattered. Winston, or Bart to his friends, walked four to five times a week, year-round, regardless of the weather.

Once a lean-mean fighting machine, his body shape had changed considerably in the decade following his war service. A man who became bored easily, he had several careers, including stints as a meteorologist, car salesperson, and even a few years as a deputy sheriff. During those early years, he learned a great deal about many things, but the less he exercised, the larger he became.

By the time he was elected to the City Council in Whitefish, Montana, in the fall of 1964, he was over two hundred and fifty pounds. Since he was well over six feet tall, he could pull it off in a well-tailored suit. But by the time he was elected as a GOP senator, he was nearing three hundred and forty pounds. And that he could not hide.

Winston Bartholomew proudly represented Montana for three terms when his first heart attack laid bare his deeper health concerns. After a quadruple bypass, he was placed on a strict diet to lose one hundred pounds, which he did. One thing about him was that if he set his mind to something, it was going to happen, and Montana loved him for his constant fight for what was right.

But in many ways, the damage to his body had been done. His knees, hips, and ankles were tired. His arthritis got far worse instead of a little better, and another mild heart attack three years later sealed the deal. At fifty-four, he called it quits and did not run for re-election.

Many tried to persuade him into a fourth term, but he was determined not to die on the job. Soon after, he began to walk with the same determination he had applied to his work.

Now, nine years later, as he walked through the light snow, his joints were stiff from the cold, but he was unphased. Almost Medicare eligible, he was a firmer two hundred and thirty pounds and able to get around without trouble.

With a propensity to vary his routine, his walks were usually two hours. He deemed that the right amount of exercise to stay in shape and recharge his marital battery. Not that Katherine, his wife of thirty-eight years, was difficult; she made few demands of him. But while he appreciated her loyalty and unyielding support, he wished she was a bit more exciting. God knows he wasn't, so he always felt he needed a stronger personality to help him, but that simply wasn't his Katherine.

Caught up in the thought, he wasn't paying attention to the ground when his boot kicked something, causing him to stumble forward. Although hardly graceful, he caught himself from going down, knowing his skeletal system would feel every bit of that tomorrow. Looking down, he noted an object unearthed by his boot when he stumbled.

The best part of hiking was the little things he came across if he was paying attention. Things like pliers, screwdrivers, wire, money, sockets from tool sets, car parts, license plates, and even a few arrowheads. The unique things he kept on his desk in a wooden bowl that he called his trophies.

He reached down to pick up his new find. It was too light to be a rock, but the weathered gray coloring was attractive. He noted the edges were highly worn, and perhaps it had been a tool at some point. His thoughts suddenly filled with images of someone using it to dig or, if sharp, using it to peel off the fat from an animal's fur. This was definitely going in the bowl.

He put the find into his pocket when a loud "snap" broke his concentration, and he looked around in all directions but saw nothing. Had he stepped on a twig? No, he thought as he glanced down. His former training told him what to look for as he glanced around again.

Several times in the last few months, he felt as if he was being watched, and it wasn't just here along the Flathead River. It had occurred in all his favorite places. It was like he was being stalked.

He had told Katherine about it, and she had suggested he talk to the local sheriff in Kalispell, Billy Jenkins. Bart had known Billy for years and gave thought to talking to him only because, as a former senator, you were bound to have offended someone. At the same time, he would only talk to Jenkins once he had something stronger than, "Hey, Sheriff, I heard a sound."

Chuckling at the absurdity of that, he kept walking.

A week passed, and he had heard no other sounds outside of nature as he pulled his Lexus SUV up to a trailhead on the east side of town. The trail itself was along the Swan River, heading away from Flathead Lake. Flat and easy, he had not hiked this one in over a year, usually opting for a few more miles, but it would work for today.

Grabbing his hiking poles, he started off, and just over a mile later, he saw a flash across the river to his right. It had been just an instantaneous white light, like the sun hitting a mirror. It also could have been the sun hitting a rifle scope or a camera lens. That was his first thought as he stopped and stared, but he saw nothing. A moment later, he heard an all-terrain vehicle, also known as a quad or ATV, traveling east from where he had seen the flash.

Most everyone here had some kind of off-road vehicle since it was part of living in a place that held more trails than roads. The most ubiquitous were quads. They could be peppy two-stroke versions or larger and quieter, four-stroke versions, and the one he just heard was an older four-stroke Honda.

He continued, but after just one loop, he elected not to do another and jumped back into his SUV. His head wasn't right, and he knew someone was trying to spook him as he drove the fifteen minutes to the Kalispell Sheriff's Station. Arriving, he walked in, and the town sheriff, Billy Jenkins, recognized him immediately.

"Hey, Bart. How the hell are you?" as he shook the man's mighty hand.

"Good, Billy, really good. Been lying low."

"Still walking, I see. You're looking good and making me feel old."

"You're very kind, Billy, but I very much feel my age. Hey, the reason I'm here is gonna sound wacky, but I think someone is following me."

He then described the last few months and the unnatural sounds, including the flash from today.

"And it's not a specific route; it can be any of them."

"Yeah, that's the damnest thing. Most days, I don't even tell Katherine where I'm going because I don't know until I do. It's kind of my thing, so hell, if I don't know, I can't imagine how anyone else does."

"Have you ever seen anyone following you when you leave the house?"

"To be honest, I've never really paid attention, but that makes sense. I guess I'll have to look around more. Be more aware."

"Yeah, do that. It's just a thought, but perhaps stop hiking for a few weeks."

Bart looked at him sharply. "No way, Billy. Nobody's going to keep me from doing what I want. It just seems weird that it occurs on at least one walk a week."

"And it's only when you're in the woods alone. Not the store, going out to eat? Any of that?"

"Nope. Only when I'm alone and on a walk."

"You carry, right?"

"Oh sure," Bart replied. Under Montana law, one could carry a registered firearm, concealed or not, without a concealed weapon permit.

"Okay, maybe wear it on your belt rather than in your pack, so it's visible and easily accessible."

"Yeah, good thinking. I will."

With that, they said their goodbyes, and Bart headed for his SUV. Once he got there, he pulled his Glock 17 from his pack and clipped it on the side of his jeans, just in case.

Chapter 2

Jenkins Residence, Kalispell

Sheriff Jenkins got home just after seven that night and cooked a burger and some potatoes on the backyard grill. He enjoyed the outdoors more than being inside, even in the cold.

When he was done, he washed it down with a beer and headed inside to warm up some, as he had to admit, the wind had a bite to it.

Jenkins had once been married, but his wife had been killed when the small plane she was flying to Whitefish crashed in foul weather. She had been the love of his life, and he couldn't bring himself to be with anyone else. Seven years later, he was still alone and likely always would be.

Clicking on the TV, he was searching for live sports when his cell phone rang. He didn't recognize the number but accepted the local call anyway, making note it was just after nine.

"Sheriff Jenkins," he said to the unknown caller.

"Billy, is that you? It's Katherine Bartholomew."

"Katherine? What are the odds? I talked to Bart earlier, and now you?"

"You talked to Bart?" she said anxiously.

"Yes, this afternoon around four. Why?"

"Did he happen to mention where he was hiking today?"

"As a matter of fact, he did. He was over by Swan River, but I got the impression he was all done. His hair looked like he'd been wearing a hat, and his gaiters were wet. What's going on, Katherine?"

"He's not come home. He likes his alone time, but it's always a few hours, not ten, and certainly not when it's dark."

Jenkins became more serious. "Okay, does he have a cell phone?"

"Yes, I've tried to call several times, but it just rings and then goes to voicemail, so I know it is on."

"You just relax and let me try to find his location from his phone. I'll let you know what I find. I'm sure it's nothing, but he could have twisted an ankle and needs some help."

"Billy, somebody has been messing with him. He told me himself."

"I know. That's why he came by today. Told me all about it. Katherine, I'm going over to the station, and I'll get back to you."

He hung up and headed for his truck.

Jenkins had been involved in a case the year prior with the local FBI, who had given him access to a program that could locate a live cell phone. Billy had used it to locate a small-time drug dealer suspected of being involved in a human trafficking operation. Rightly or wrongly, they had never altered his credentials, so he still had access to the application.

A cellphone produces a time-stamped record every time it connects to a cell tower. Jenkins wasn't interested in the phone data itself, only the ability to see where the phone had been recently. For that, he didn't require a warrant if he had a reasonable cause. Since Bart had described a plausible threat five hours earlier and was now several hours past due, it seemed all he needed.

Arriving at the station, he logged into the system and typed in Bart's cell phone number. The program would disclose nothing about the phone or its contents, but it would give its last known location. He watched the screen when it popped up. The phone was near the Swan River trailhead.

He quickly phoned Katherine Bartholomew and told her Bart's phone was at Swan River but for her to stay put, and he was heading there now. He would call her later. She wanted to meet him there, but he said no until he could find out why he wasn't answering his phone.

Both understood what he meant. He hung up concerned, and she hung up crying.

Jenkins quickly unlocked the station's gun locker, grabbed a Mossberg shotgun, and stuffed five rounds into the magazine tube. Heading out to his truck, he placed the shotgun into the truck's gun lock before racing to the river with his emergency lights off. Few cars were out, as folks here tended to rise early and bed down early.

As he approached the river trailhead, he slowed and entered the dirt parking area, turning on his spotlight. The bright glow immediately captured Bart's Lexus SUV, and Billy jumped out and approached it with a worried look. Shing a light into the locked car, on the seat was a cell phone. This wasn't good.

From his truck, he called the two deputies that made up his station and told them to meet him at the trailhead. He also called a close friend of four years, Richard Chase.

When he first met Chase, he tried to recruit him into the Kalispell Sheriff's Department. However, Chase, new to Montana, had other ideas and ended up opening a boutique security company called Fortitude Security. Although they specialized in private security, Chase, a former Navy SEAL, was fearless, and often worked with Jenkins and his small department.

Everyone was present when Jenkins sent the two deputies, Ben Mcloud and Scott Thompson, down the trail while he and Chase headed east. That was the approximate area where Bart had said he thought he saw a scope flash earlier that day. As far as Billy was concerned, it might be nothing, or it might be everything, as he glanced at his watch showing a quarter past ten.

Jenkins and Chase crossed the river on a small wooden bridge a mile down the trail and headed in the general direction Bart had mentioned. The forest here was extremely thick, and with nothing to slow its growth, moving forward was not for the faint of heart.

Soon, the forest leveled out, and in the muddy tundra, the tracks of an ATV were spotted in the light of Jenkins' headlamp. The tire tracks were recent, and Jenkins followed them right, and Chase went left.

It wasn't ten minutes later when Chase, who had headed upriver, yelled, "Billy, head towards my light. We have a problem."

Jenkins immediately turned towards his voice and held the shotgun loosely in both hands as he retraced his steps toward Chase. Sadly, he had a pretty good idea of what the problem was. He noted the light from Chase's headlamp and followed it like a beacon.

Slowing as he caught up with him, Jenkins clicked on the safety of the Mossberg. There was little need for it now.

On the ground in front of Chase was the body of Winston "Bart" Bartholomew.

Chapter 3

Swan River Trail, Bigfork, Day One

As the clock turned past midnight, portable lights had turned the dark forest and meadow into near daylight. The yellowish light from the gas-powered units bled over the top of the pop-up tent that deputies Mcloud and Thompson had placed around the body. This was to help preserve evidence, but the artificial light left dark shadows behind the tent itself. It was there that they were met by the local Crime Scene team from Kalispell, who had just arrived.

The town of Bigfork was located in Flathead County, and the county seat was in Kalispell. The county coroner was located there, although the district office was in Missoula, eighty miles south. The coroner himself, Dr. William Kingman, wasn't there yet but was expected given the notoriety of the victim.

The CSI leading the team was Cheyenne Denton, a descendant of the Kalispel Indians who had lived here for over two hundred years. Today, they and two other tribes called the Flathead Indian Reservation home, and Cheyenne herself was no stranger to a crime scene.

Billy and Richard had just walked toward the tent when she walked out and snapped off a pair of gloves with a loud snap. "Hey guys."

An amazing woman in every respect, Cheyenne was taller than average, with a toned muscular shape and hard-chiseled features of her American Indian heritage. Add that to a smart, educated mind and her ability to bounce from tomboy to prom queen depending on the company, made for a complete package.

Jenkins took the lead. "Hey, Cheyenne. I know it's early, but anything of note outside the obvious?"

"You mean that ten-inch knife sticking out of his heart. Pretty much as it looks, Billy. Kingman will have to rule, but it looks like cause of death. There are no other obvious signs of trauma and no defensive wounds, although there are a couple of oddities."

"Like his empty gun holster?"

"That is one, and come daylight, we'll try to find it. What I was going to say was that when I completed the standard fingernail swab, I also checked for gunshot residue. The field test was affirmative."

"So, he recently fired a gun."

"Within hours."

"Time of death?"

"Just starting to see rigor mortis, so between seven and nine tonight is my best guess."

"Anything else?"

"Yes, from every angle, the position of the body is inconsistent with a stab wound in the center of his chest. Unlikely, he was stabbed where he was found."

Chase nodded. "I saw that. Looks more like he was dumped there."

"Maybe from an ATV," Jenkins said, glancing down at the tire tracks.

Cheyenne flashed her light right and left. "I'll get a team on that." Her phone buzzed, and she glanced at the message. "Hey, guys, heads up. Kingman will be here in an hour."

Turning back to go back inside, she looked at Richard, smiled, and gave him the universal "Call me" sign with her left hand and a little curtsy. Cheyenne had the hots for him, although he was trying to avoid acknowledging it.

Chase ignored the gesture and turned to Jenkins, "This is murder."

Jenkins frowned. "Yep. It's hard enough to lose an icon like Bart Bartholomew, but Kalispell is going to be swarming with every fucking agency in the US of A by noon tomorrow. It's going to be long days ahead."

As he said the words, Chase only nodded.

Shortly after talking to Cheyenne, Billy left the scene to give the news to Katherine Bartholomew. Richard had offered to join him, but Billy felt it would be best if he were alone since he had known the Bartholomews since they moved here in the eighties.

The Bartholomews lived on the edge of town in a small community of large, gated houses. As he arrived at their house, he used an emergency services code to enter their gate. The house was set far back on the property as he drove slowly up the circular driveway. The porch lights came on as soon as he pulled up, and Katherine answered the door the moment he knocked. Fully clothed, she had not been sleeping, but seemed to droop when she saw him.

"Hi," she said quietly, as her voice cracked. "I assume you wouldn't be here at midnight if the news was positive."

Another woman came forward and put her hand around Katherine's shoulder.

Jenkins eyed her and said, "Ma'am."

"Hello, Sheriff Jenkins, I'm Angie. I live next door and have been with Katherine since she called you."

"That is very kind of you. Can we take this inside?"

Momentarily unaware of the cold air, Katherine suddenly understood and replied, "Of course, I'm sorry."

They entered, followed by Billy, who closed the door. They all went into the spacious living room, and Katherine began to cry.

"Can I get you a coffee, Billy?" Katherine asked, trying to hold it together.

He looked down and then back up. In a calm voice, he replied, "No thanks. Katherine. Listen, I'm so very sorry, but when we found Bart deceased."

"Did he kill himself?" she asked.

Her reply shocked him, though he tried not to react, although both women were looking at him as if that was precisely what they suspected. Taken aback, he said in disbelief, "What? Why would you say that?"

His widow of less than a minute replied, "It's just so late, and he has been gone for sixteen hours. We just thought, I mean Angie thought maybe, he might have killed himself."

"Was he prone to such thoughts? Did he ever mention being depressed and wanting to take his life?" Jenkins asked, unsure.

"Well, no, he said nothing like that. He's just been so different lately. So distant."

"How so?"

The neighbor, Angie, said immediately, "Over the last few years, he has been detached, especially around Katherine. Depressed is what I thought."

"Katherine, would you agree with that statement?"

"Yes."

Jenkins paused to find the words. "Well, I'm sorry for that, but nothing I saw would indicate he had taken his own life."

"Was he found in his car?" The neighbor asked.

"No." He said to her before turning to Katherine, "He was found off-trail next to Swan River."

"At this hour?"

The neighbor then asked, "Was he shot?"

Jenkins ignored her and looked at Katherine. "The investigation is just getting underway, and I think it's best not to speculate further until the forensic team completes their job."

"But you said his wounds were not self-inflected, so if you await details from CSI, then he was most certainly murdered," Angie said matter-of-factly.

Katherine yelped and as Billy went toward her, Angie wrapped her arms around her as if to protect her.

He stopped in his tracks and couldn't explain why the neighbor bothered him, but the damn woman certainly wasn't helping.

"I'm sorry, Katherine, but I don't have any other information at this time. For peace of mind, I'll have a car parked in your driveway tonight."

Neither woman said a thing, although Katherine nodded. Jenkins looked to the neighbor, "You'll be able to stay with her?"

"Yes, of course."

Putting on his hat, he said, "Thanks for that. Katherine, other than his office, where were his most private places here in the house?"

"I can only think of his office. Oh, and the room behind the garage." She said, puzzled, before adding, "Why?"

"As part of our investigation protocols, we'll be back at daybreak with a small team to check those places out."

"Is that necessary? I mean, he wasn't killed here," she said, not at all happy with the thought.

"Katherine, whatever happened, it happened for a reason, although we don't know what that is just yet. These rooms could contain evidence to help us understand, so if it is all right, I'm going to seal off those two rooms now. From this moment forward, only the CSI team can go inside. At least until both rooms are cleared."

Angie had been trying to open her mouth and suddenly blurted out, "That is ridiculous. This is her house. She can go wherever she wants."

"Ma'am, I was not directing the question toward you."

Her mouth closed as she took a step back.

Katherine said softly, "Billy, I understand what you're trying to say, and I trust you. I'll be ready the best I can, and yes, you may seal the rooms. I have no desire to be in them, anyway."

"Thank you, Katherine, and I'll see you in a few hours. Try to get some sleep."

"Sheriff, are you going back to the crime scene," Angie asked.

"I'll be right back," he said.

As he walked out into the frosty night to get his sealing kit, the door closed behind him. The sobs of Katherine Bartholomew were easily heard through the door as he headed for his truck.

It was another forty minutes before he made it back into the crime scene with some gas station coffee and handed a cup to Chase as he walked up.

Chase nodded in thanks and asked, "How is she?"

"She almost seemed to have expected the news and even asked me if he killed himself," looking at Chase, perplexed.

"Bart. Suicide. She really said that?"

"Swear to God, but I think her nutty neighbor has been filling her head with nonsense. There's something not right about her."

Chapter 4

Swan River Trail, Bigfork

The earlier comments from Cheyenne regarding Dr. Kingman's arrival had been meant as a warning. Just moments later, the gruff sound of his voice filled the quiet.

"Standing around drinking coffee. Wonderful. So much for the integrity of my crime scene," Kingman bellowed.

Jenkins looked at his watch unperturbed. "Please note, Dr. Kingman, there are no reporters or bystanders. I would say we have effectively preserved your scene. Although I couldn't help but notice you're not wearing shoe covers, a Tyvek suit, or gloves. Further, you have wandered outside the police tape and are now standing on the tracks of an ATV. The same vehicle, we believe, brought the victim here, and likely is how the murderer left. Feel free to stop by the station tomorrow, so I might remind you of our field protocols."

Kingman turned red and, in a huff, headed toward the tent, where he placed covers on his shoes and put on gloves before entering. It was fifteen minutes before he emerged with Cheyenne.

"I understand Ms. Denton has brought you up to speed," Kingman proclaimed.

"She did. Anything to add?"

"No, we need daylight. Protect the scene, as the swarm will no doubt arrive soon."

"When will you transport?" Chase asked.

Kingman replied, "They'll be here in twenty minutes. We'll need some help to lift him without damaging the area around the body. I'm going to take him to our office here in Kalispell, but I can't start the examination until the

FBI arrives. Apparently, they want to send his remains to Missoula for forensics."

"They've already contacted you?" Jenkins asked, surprised.

"Yes, just before I arrived. For your sake, I hope you have been as thorough as you claim."

"Not our first rodeo, Dr. Kingman. Let me know when you get the okay," Jenkins responded, unphased by his attempt to challenge him.

"Why? In a few hours, you'll no longer be running the show."

With that, Kingman smugly walked away to meet with the transport team, who would soon be across the river. The local ranger must have already opened the gate so the van could drive the mile to the footbridge.

Chase shook his head. Kingman was a pompous ass who either had no clue how he came off or didn't care what anyone thought of him.

It was close to five that morning when Jenkins and Chase left the scene to return to the sheriff's station. They compared notes, and after an hour, Chase headed home while Jenkins readied himself to meet with the two CSIs at the Bartholomew house.

When they arrived, Katherine was there to greet them. The officer remained in the driveway, and a second was positioned outside the gate. It would be just hours before the sleepy town caught wind of what had happened and descended onto the cul-de-sac.

"Morning Katherine," he said as the neighbor, Angie, came alongside her and gave him a stare. Jenkins ignored her.

"Can we go somewhere private?"

"Of course, follow me," Angie said.

"Ma'am, I appreciate your kindness, but nothing I have to say pertains to you. Katherine, if you can lead the way."

"But I need to be there to support her," Angie pleaded.

"Noted, and thanks, but this does not concern you. Katherine, may we." He motioned forward, and they went into the study. Katherine sat on the couch as he closed the door and joined her.

"Katherine, Bart was murdered, and his remains are with our local ME, but the FBI will soon be here to take jurisdiction."

"They can do that?"

"Yes, ma'am."

"So, someone shot him."

"For now, someone took his life. While the CSI team reviews the crime scene, I have several questions. Can we speak here?"

"Yes. Can Angie come in?"

"I think it would be best for her not to be here," Jenkins said as nicely as he could muster before adding, "May I ask why you wish her here?"

"She knows a great deal about criminology and has been helping me to understand."

"Understand what?"

"What happens now?" Katherine replied.

"Is she a criminologist?"

"No, I don't think so. I fancied her as an amateur sleuth."

Just great, Jenkins thought as he rolled his eyes.

"Katherine, we're early in our investigation, and I have just a few hours to coordinate our facts before this turns into a full-blown circus. The Feds don't mean it to happen that way, but inevitably, it does. I would ask for your help to let me ask my questions."

"Go ahead, I'm sorry."

"Don't be sorry. I know a thing or two about loss," he replied, and she nodded, knowing his own situation when his wife was killed.

"Can you think of any reason someone would want to harm your husband?"

"No. I mean, everyone loved him."

"Everyone? He was a councilman and a senator. That is a lot of opportunity to please some and anger others."

"But I don't know those people. None came forward, and the only threat I'm aware of was well over fourteen years ago."

"Tell me about it," Jenkins replied.

"Bart ran for Senate when Max passed away."

"I recall that."

She was referring to Max Robinson, the former Senator of Montana.

"Max had backed a bill to restrict certain forms of aid to Vietnam Veterans who had committed a felony. When Bart won, it came to vote, and rather than researching the legal case, he thought it best to vote in favor as Max would have wished. He got a threat the day after."

"How were the threats received?"

"Single sheets with cut and pasted words out of magazines. The Secret Service took them, but Bart had copies. I can get them for you. They are in his office."

"Okay. We'll grab them later. What happened then?"

"A man was convicted."

"I'll look up the case. Anyone else?"

"Not that I recall."

"Anything threats more recently?"

"No."

"Okay. Are you the sole beneficiary of his estate?"

"Yes."

"You didn't have children. Are there any relatives who might contest his trust?"

"Bart never talked about his family outside of his own mother and father. He had a sister, but she died when he was running for the city council seat."

"How did she die?"

"An accident. She was an avid cyclist and was killed in Whitefish," she said as Jenkins made notes.

"So, no other family? Aunts, Uncles?"

"Not that I'm aware of."

"You said Bart was acting 'off.' Did that behavior start after any particular event? A fight or argument?"

"No. He has always been stoic but was happy in his own way. He could even be gregarious around others. It was only with me he seemed sad."

"Trouble with the marriage?"

"I don't think so. I mean, we've been married for decades. It was just painfully obvious that he was especially solemn around me, so there was something about me he didn't care for."

"How long has it been like this?"

"Maybe twenty years."

Jenkins looked at her, flabbergasted. "That's a long time, Katherine. Did you two ever talk about it?"

"No. I asked once if he was mad at me, and he just said he wished I was happier. He said he liked a happy house, whatever in the hell that meant."

"But you didn't question him?"

"Of course not. I have always been comfortable in the role of the lonely wife."

"Lonely wife?" he asked, somewhat confused.

"Billy, you must recall, Bart traveled three weeks a month, and I was rarely invited to go with him. So yes, seeing your husband one week a month was lonely. When he retired, I thought it would improve, but he just took up hobbies that kept him away from me. That seemed to be what he wanted."

Katherine started to cry. As Billy handed her a tissue, he thought perhaps that was enough for now. They were both interrupted by a knock on the door, and Jenkins rose and opened it to find one of his deputies.

"Sheriff, we got at least a dozen reporters outside the gate trying to get in. We're gonna need some backup."

Jenkins turned to her. "Katherine, these reporters want a story, and they don't much care if it hurts you while they try to create it. If it were me, I would leave town, but if that is not possible, get hold of your family attorney and explain the situation. He can create some legal protections to help you, but I'll get more guys until the cavalry comes. I'm going to touch base with the forensics team, talk to your neighbor, and then head back to the station to meet with the FBI. Call me if you need anything."

"I will, and thank you, Billy. You've always been a good friend. I just can't believe someone killed him."

He nodded and walked out of the room to meet the neighbor, Angie.

"Ma'am, can I have your full name?"

"Is Katherine okay?"

Ignoring her, he asked again, "Your surname, please."

"Griffin is my married name. My maiden name is Taylor."

He noted the four-caret diamond on her finger. "Griffin, as in Mark Griffin, the developer."

"The same."

"Are you with law enforcement?"

Whatever he might have said, nothing could have pleased her more.

"No. But as you have noted, Detective, I have a keen mind for crime."

"I'm the county sheriff, not a detective. So, you're a criminal then?"

"What? No. Of course not." She replied in horror. "We have money. Why would I steal anything?"

"The word criminal is a generic term for all crimes, Ms. Griffin."

"Well, I am not one and cannot believe that was your first reaction," she snipped, clearly offended.

"So, your keen mind for crime is not because you take part but because you like it?"

"Oh yes. Very much so. I'm going to write a novel about a murder, so I spend a great deal of time studying murderers and the people who chase them."

"I see . . ." Jenkins got off before she blurted out.

"Please call me Angie. By the way, I would love to pick your brain about how you operate and get details to help my main character. I'm going to name him 'Agent Zack Zamora,' catchy, right? Dinner, perhaps?"

"Ms. Griffin, I'm afraid I will not have much of a life for the next month, and it would be inappropriate for me to do so. I have a request, however. Katherine is in a vulnerable state. It is important that you do not fill her head with conspiracy theories in your attempt to wow her with your amazing knowledge. It will only confuse her about what law enforcement is doing to help find what really happened to her husband."

"So, he wasn't murdered."

"Please, Ms. Griffin. I'm quite serious."

"But I was convinced he was murdered."

"Why?"

"Katherine didn't tell you?"

"Tell me what."

"He was having an affair."

"An affair?"

"Oh yes. Winston and my husband are, I mean were, in business together. I heard all about it from some of my husband's employees."

Showing no other emotions, Jenkins replied, "Tell your husband to contact me," as he handed her his business card. No sooner had he done so than his phone went off.

"Jenkins," he said as he listened to the request. He sighed and said, "I'm on my way."

"Ms. Griffin, please keep what we discussed to yourself until we can verify the story, and we'll talk again. Have you discussed this with Katherine?"

"No. I wanted to, but it's not my place, although I guess it would just be hurtful to say something now."

"I agree. I have to meet with the FBI."

"Oh wow, how exciting. Can I come? I could be Katherine's liaison."

"I think we have it covered, Ms. Griffin," he said as he brought his hat back to his head and headed out the door. He wasn't sure what was worse, Angie Griffin or the FBI agent that was sure to ruin his day.

Chapter 5

Chase Residence, Kalispell

"Richard Chase speaking," he said, half asleep, as he poured a cup of rich black coffee and simultaneously answered his house phone. It was nearing nine, and he had decided it was better to just go on with his day rather than try to sleep for a few hours. Nevertheless, he felt absolutely trashed.

"Mr. Chase, this is Katherine Bartholomew. I hope you remember me?"

Surprised at the call, he replied, "Katherine, of course I remember you and I'm so sorry for your loss, we're all shocked. Is Billy there?"

"No, he just left. I believe the FBI is waiting for him at his station."

"Is everything okay?"

"Yes, I mean no. Nothing is really okay, is it? And my quiet street. It is no longer and presently overrun with reporters. My poor neighbors are going to hate me."

"Annoyed, maybe, but I suspect they would do anything for you. Reach out to them; friends can help. What can I do for you, Katherine?"

Chase set down his coffee, realizing if he had any more, he was going to get the jitters from too much caffeine.

"Were you there? I mean, when they found him?" She asked.

"Yes. Billy and I found him."

"He was murdered?"

"Katherine, when I'm with Billy, I am deputized. I can't comment about last night."

"I understand, but Billy told me as such, although he refuses to say how he was killed. I'm just looking for answers."

"I can understand that, but it really has just been hours since the discovery."

"Perhaps. In any event, the reason I called is that I wish to hire your company to find out who killed my husband. Money is no object."

"Katherine, between today and tomorrow, the FBI will be descending on Bigfork, and they'll quickly find out what happened."

"Mr. Chase, I don't trust most in Government or the FBI, and ironically, neither did Bart. I'm fond of Billy, but he will need help with this."

"Why do you think that?"

"Mark my words. Whatever is going on, it's much larger than my husband."

"Katherine, let a few days pass, and then we can talk again."

"Fair enough," she replied, and the call ended.

Chase was thinking to himself, *what the hell was that about,* as he set down the phone. Jenkins called just minutes later.

Richard picked by and asked, "Hey Billy, I heard the Feds were in town?"

"Yeah. You better head over. I'll be there in fifteen minutes."

"Okay, on my way."

"Don't come to my station. Go straight to the FBI office on Main."

"Okay," Richard said with a yawn.

The FBI Resident Agency for Flathead County was built in the late 1970s, and from the street, it could easily have passed as a bank. The modern single-story structure wasn't huge, although the territory the agency covered was. Chase arrived just as Jenkins pulled in. They shook hands and walked in to see ten people hustling around the inner spaces. Standing in front of that was a shorter man, at least compared to Chase and Jenkins. He stood stick straight, in his late thirties, possibly early forties, and everything about him screamed he was a Federal Agent.

He turned to them without an expression, and his eyes settled on Richard.

"You, Jenkins?" the FBI agent asked of Richard.

"No sir, Richard Chase, Fortitude Security."

"And what are you doing here?"

"Billy and I found the body," Chase said as he glanced at Billy, who already disliked this agent.

Jenkins stiffened and asked, "I'm Sheriff Jenkins and who do we have the pleasure of working with."

"Special Agent Jeremy Stone. Mr. Chase, you may leave. It is hard enough to cooperate with local police. I hardly need a rent-a-cop to make it worse."

Jenkins jumped before Chase.

"He's not going anywhere, Agent Stone, and you can stop with your mightier-than-oak attitude. When I call Chase to assist me, he is deputized under Montana law, so he is, for all practical purposes, an extension of my office."

"Sheriff, we'll try this again. You work for me. I do not work for you. Bring me up to speed on the Senator."

Jenkins pulled out a thin manilla folder representing the first six hours of the Bartholomew case he had been carrying under his arm.

"Former Senator and I assume you can read," as he plopped the small file down on the desk in front of the Special Agent.

Somewhere, this office was the Special Agent in Charge (SAIC), but that person had not yet made an appearance. Stone gave him a glare and grabbed the file, saying nothing as he methodically read each page carefully. Five or six minutes passed when he looked up and asked, "Reactions?"

Jenkins replied. "As you read, Bart had been spooked over the last few months and finally came to me yesterday. He heard odd sounds and sights that only occurred when he was walking by himself. With no other specifics, I told him to stop his walks, but he refused. It would now appear he returned to the area where he thought he saw a scope flash or a camera lens flash and was murdered."

"His gun has not been found?"

"No, but a preliminary report from CSI says there was gunshot residue on his hand. He fired his gun last night."

"Is the CSI team from Kalispell or Missoula?"

"Kalispell."

"And they are also searching for blood or another body?"

"Yes, that is already in progress, in addition to locating the missing gun."

"What about these comments regarding body position?"

"Richard and I noted that his body looked dumped. The CSI Lead confirmed the body location was inconsistent with a frontal wound. Her report is forthcoming as she is still at the scene. We also located fresh ATV tracks leading to and from the body, and we have another team working on that now."

"What about you, hotshot?" as Stone glanced toward Chase.

"Are you talking to me, Agent Stone?"

"Yes, I am."

"Wasn't sure, name isn't Hot Shot," Richard said just to piss him off.

"Save it, Mr. Chase. I'm aware of your vigilante justice business. Thoughts?"

Chase would not let this asshole get him riled and answered professionally. "Bart wasn't a small guy, and he knew how to fight. Whoever killed him was a friend."

Stone looked up. "And what makes you say that?"

"Like us, he had very specific training. That means that only someone close to him could ever get close enough to stab him in the chest without receiving significant defensive wounds. To that end, there was no secondary blood at the dumping point. And even if Bart got off a shot, the murderer was strong enough to get his dead weight onto an ATV."

"Unless there was more than one assailant," Stone snapped, happy with himself as he turned to Jenkins. Switching gears, he asked, "You were with his widow earlier. What was that like?"

"They possibly had some marital issues, and she thought he had been more depressed than normal. To her knowledge, the only known threat he ever received was fifteen years ago. They got a conviction. I'll get the name and investigate the guy's status."

"I'll cover it." Stone then asked, "If they were having marital problems, he might have strayed?"

"Needs to be looked into," Jenkins replied with remorse.

"Okay. Let's populate the evidence board." They all started to follow Stone when he turned to Richard. "Mr. Chase, your services are no longer required."

"No problem," Chase said, to Jenkins' surprise, as he turned and headed for his truck. Jenkins would call him later.

Stone turned to the Sheriff. "If that cowboy's name shows up during this investigation, arrest him. Clear?"

Jenkins ignored him, and for the next hour, they populated the board with magnetic cards that you could write on. At one point, Jenkins' phone buzzed, and he stepped out to answer it. It was Deputy Thompson. Jenkins listened for a few minutes and then said, "You guys stay at the crime scene and help Cheyenne and her team. When you're done there, stop by and help keep the press away from the Bartholomew house."

When he reentered, Stone said in a condescending tone, "Something more important that finding our killer Sheriff?"

"Stone, you're an asshole, and that chip on your shoulder needs to settle down. Winston Bartholomew was my damn friend, and nobody in my office will rest until we find his killer. There are significant resources at your disposal, but if you keep pissing them off, you'll find yourself alone in a county that has no love for the federal government."

"Sheriff, if you think we are not fully trained to work without local support in far-right states, you are sadly mistaken."

"Fine, I tried. It won't be my ass they fire when you fail."

Stone looked at him smugly. "And you are so very wrong, Sheriff."

Chapter 6

Chase Residence, Kalispell

Chase returned to the cabin and nodded to Manny Vasquez, his only full-time employee outside of Fortitude Security. Manny had briefly been an Army Ranger but was discharged due to conduct, and Richard hired him a year later, giving him a purpose. He had also paid for anger management therapy. Manny would be anything for Richard.

"Hey Manny, did Nate get off to school?"

He was referring to his eleven-year-old son, Nathen, who liked to be called Nate these days.

"Sure. He didn't want to take the bus and rode his mountain bike. How is Billy?"

"He's gonna lose some sleep over this one. Losing Bart is one thing. But this FBI Agent Stone is a real asshole."

"Surprised you're not there."

"I was, but was asked to leave. Stone said he didn't want a 'rent-a-cop' clouding things up."

"And he's still breathing?" Vasquez said with a smirk.

"Thought crossed my mind," as Chase headed to his home office.

Although Kalispell schools had bus service, Nate preferred to ride his bike, and Richard wasn't at all concerned. Nate was a great kid, a good student, and a solid athlete.

Maybe because he never had a choice as a boy, Richard allowed his son to make most of all his own decisions, even at eleven. The only prerequisite was that he had to maintain a grade point average of 3.5 or higher. That was because he and Darna had only created one mandate. Their son was college-bound, whether he wanted it or not.

That rationale was simple. First, his mom, Darna, was a college graduate, the first in her family. Second, when Richard left his family's farm, he worked hard to get his general educational development test before becoming a Navy SEAL. Physicality was never an issue, but math and science were difficult for him with his limited education.

Although he would eventually get an undergraduate degree thanks to the US Government, it wasn't easy, and his base of knowledge was still overwhelmingly real-life over academics. He wanted a different life for Nate.

In Richard's view, his job was to be better than his dad. By extension, that meant it was Nate's job to be better than Richard, and he intended to make the boy work for that honor.

Later that day, Jenkins reviewed the CSI findings of the sweep of Bartholomew's office and a room off the garage. Both locations revealed little although there were a few things about Bart, previously unknown.

In the room off the garage, Bart was apparently a cigar smoker who liked fine wine and rare whiskey. His collection was superior, and based on the recycling bins; this wasn't just an occasional pastime. It also meant he spent considerable time there and enjoyed this with others–there were too many bottles for it to be just him.

There was no porn, few books, a couple of hiking magazines, and only a handful of photos of him and Katherine. The thing they found of possible significance was a journal he kept of his hikes, which they would go through thoroughly.

In his home office, they discovered he was far more into real estate and investing than Jenkins could have imagined and was doing very well. No less than six million dollars of current investments.

They located the project Angie Griffin had mentioned, a high-end condo project on the east side of Flathead Lake. It had taken eight years to gain approval from the city council and local tribal leaders, and many who had opposed it. Jenkins would talk to Mark Griffin and determine if enemies could be found there.

Oddly, the condo project was the only one that carried Winston's real name. All others contained the codename, "Phoenix," which begged the question, why was he hiding his name, and who was the attorney who handled such things for him? They found no record of either.

Billy needed to talk to Katherine, so he made his way to the house. When he arrived, he had to proceed slowly through a maze of reporters standing in the street at the end of the cul-de-sac. Waving to Deputy Thompson, he promptly entered the gate.

As he drove to the house in the daylight, the property was magnificent, and it was easy to understand why Bart had chosen this place as his forever home. Stopping on the circular drive, he stepped out of the truck, and when he neared the door, it opened, and Katherine was there.

"Hello Billy, I saw you driving up."

"Is Ms. Griffin inside?" he replied, hoping the answer was no.

"She left, but will be back. Should we wait for her?"

"No, we should not."

"Then, please come in."

"Thanks," as he took off his hat and entered. "Katherine, I have a few questions following our search of Bart's personal rooms."

"Oh dear. I always wondered what he did there."

"It's nothing like that. The spaces were fine, although there were a few oddities that I wanted to ask you about. Is that alright?"

"Of course, although I may be as surprised as yourself. We didn't communicate much. Those rooms were part of his way not to be with me."

"We'll get back to that. In the room next to the garage, he had a cigar bar."

"Yes, he enjoyed a nice cigar."

"Did he entertain there, other guys? Poker night?"

"Yes, sometimes."

Jenkins nodded. "In his office we located a great deal of investment material. Bart was quite active."

"I know he had a business venture with Mark Griffin and a few odds and ends, but nothing serious."

"The investments we have are worth over six million dollars."

"What? We have money, but not that kind of money." Katherine replied.

"Well, you do. Let's continue. On his desk was a bowl of trinkets. What do those represent?"

"The wood bowl?"

"Yes."

"Those were items he found as he hiked."

"One of them was a possible Indian artifact."

"Oh yes, the arrowheads. Those were his favorite."

"No, I was referring to a piece of human bone."

"Bone? What do you mean?"

"There was a gray-colored piece. It looked like a scoop. The pathologist in Kalispell said it was a human bone."

"Perhaps it is another piece from the Kalispel Tribe that once occupied this land."

"Could be. So, you weren't aware of it?"

"No, he usually showed me, but not that one."

"Very well. We also found a hiking journal."

"You mean like a guidebook?"

"No. It was his notes from each hike. There were four volumes."

"I had no idea, but I would love to see them. I mean, they're mine, right?"

"Yes, of course. For now, they are evidence. He may have detailed an event that could be construed as a threat."

"I see. Well, make sure they are not destroyed. I am very much interested in what he thought during his twenty-plus hours a week in the woods."

"You have my word." Billy stopped for a second. "Katherine, this is difficult, but you mentioned he was not always attentive to you and even acted differently around you. Was there perhaps another woman?"

She stiffened, and her face went from worry to outright fury. "How could you even say that?"

"Katherine, I'm just doing my job. I'm not saying he did or didn't. I'm just asking."

"Did you find something to suggest this?"

"No. It is just standard inquiry."

"Well, it is unfair and rude."

"Katherine, please, I just had to ask. Better me than the FBI, right?"

"No. It's not better because I don't know them and can assume they are assholes. But you, you're a family friend!"

Jenkins snapped, "Who had no idea you were having marital issues? Katherine, right now, everyone is a suspect, and I assure you that will be the FBI's take."

"Including me?" she said in horror.

"Yes."

Shortly after, Jenkins was shown the door. He felt bad, but had he not closed that lead, the FBI would push her to the limit. He didn't really suspect her in the least, but Chase's comment to Agent Stone that the murderer was a friend rang true to him.

He had just entered his truck when Richard called.

"Billy, you have a few minutes."

"Yeah, I was just leaving Katherine."

"Should I ask?"

"No. What do you have?"

"It's about the affair that Angie Griffin spoke of. Apparently, there was a reception for the Condo project in Lakeside."

"Lakeside?"

"Yes. It was at the Harbor Grill in Harbor Marina. Griffin threw a party to celebrate after they received approval. We spoke to a server there who recalls the event, and according to her, an attractive, very intoxicated woman was there trying to wrap herself around Bart. That said, he was having none of it, and a security guard asked her to leave. I don't think he was having an affair. Likely just a gold-digger."

"Okay, thanks. Find a name if you can. I'm headed over to talk with Mark Griffin now. I'll get his take."

Chase was out on the rear porch later that evening, overlooking a small lake he used for irrigation and runoff. Having a rye old-fashioned, the sound of a car on the gravel drive came to a stop and brought a weak smile to his exhausted face. He surmised it was Jenkins who had driven his Subaru Outback over, leaving the Sheriff's truck at the station. Chase listened as the door opened, and soon after, Jenkins came into the house, poured himself a few fingers of scotch, and headed out to the fire pit.

"Eternal day. I'm wiped!" he said as he sat down across from Richard.

"Right there with you."

"You were a good boy today. Shocked the crap out of me. Even the kids were impressed." He sometimes referred to deputies Mcloud and Thompson as the kids. Not that Richard, at thirty-five, and he, at forty-one were old, but their experiences certainly aged them significantly over the two deputies.

"How did it go with Mark Griffin?"

"He wasn't home, and Ms. Griffin wasn't sure where he was. I called him, though, and we agreed to talk tomorrow."

Richard nodded. "Before I forget or fall asleep, I got a call this morning from Katherine Bartholomew."

"Really, why?"

"She wants to hire Fortitude to feed you information. Money is no object, she said."

"You're messing with me, right?" unsure what to make of the news.

"No. I told her to let a few days pass before we spoke again, so we are not under contract, but I'll probably agree to work behind the scenes. The Feds have significant resources, but they won't get there as fast as we can."

Billy replied, "I didn't hear this conversation, but our friend Stone said, and this is a quote. If that cowboy shows up at any time in this investigation, we're to arrest you."

Richard reached over and held up his glass, which he clicked to Billy's.

"In for a penny. In for a pound." He was referring to an expression from the 1600s that was an admonition against crimes for debt. The meaning was simple, if one owed another just one penny, it did not differ from owing someone a pound. Same punishment.

Chapter 7

Fortitude Security, Kalispell, Day Two

The next morning, after some much-needed rest, Richard walked to the barn that housed Fortitude. It was next door to the cabin on the twenty acres he owned although it wasn't a barn at all. It might look like a barn from the outside, but was a well-appointed office building inside. One that now housed six researchers and analysts, and it looked new because it was.

Two years before, a team of mercenaries had been sent to Fortitude to destroy it and everything in it, including Richard and his team. Thankfully, he outmaneuvered them and, in turn, blew them all up along with the barn. He and Nate had just rebuilt it the year before.

Although Richard was a former Navy SEAL and excelled at action, that was not the true secret of Fortitudes' success. What set SEALs and Rangers apart was superior training and the quality of their intelligence. All soldiers needed intel on what they were up against, and the military analysts behind them provided the intel to keep them alive.

So, when Richard started Fortitude, he partnered with Jenkins to locate minds that could see through the coding and logic that made computers and search engines work. These kids were explorers of the digital world, and while Richard had no idea what they did, he hired the best of them.

Walking into a small office that housed his very first employee at Fortitude sat a lanky, unkept twenty-one-year-old named Eddy Laughlin. He was typing away, trying to understand the partner relationships behind Conrad Point Estates.

"Morning Eddy, what do you have."

"Not ready."

Chase replied firmly, "Get ready. I need to update Jenkins before noon."

Eddy was loyal as all hell, but while talented, you had to manhandle him a bit. He never liked to share until he had all the facts, and sometimes, that became too late for the client or the situation.

Eddy just nodded and gave his textbook reply. "On it."

Richard left and went to his other primary resource, Alex Alexander. Unlike Eddy, who took no pride in his appearance, Alex looked fresh out of prep school, but her looks were deceiving. Alex was not just a solid programmer. She was also a seasoned analyst and often worked in the field. Her appearance and mannerisms put most people at ease, and they usually talked to her far more than they should. She and Eddy had broken open some wild cases over the last three years.

"Alex, you're looking radiant this morning. Anything yet?"

She smiled and replied, "The program is still running, but I should have a rough view later today."

Alex had scanned Bart's hiking logbooks before Jenkins was forced to hand them over to the FBI. Soon after, she had written a computer program that searched for keywords involving danger, threats, or fear.

"What are our chances?" Richard asked.

"Not sure. We have two constraints. First is that Mr. Bartholomew sometimes wrote as he was walking, so his handwriting is not uniform. That makes it hard for the print recognition software to grab the correct letters. Second, he writes like I imagine you would. What might scare the piss out of me is no big deal to you. So, the keywords I would use don't directly compare to those you or he seemed to use. We'll have to see. So far, I have a lot of hits, but they have turned out to be false flags once I actually read the text. Come back in a few hours."

"Okay, thanks. Of the four logs, I'm most interested in the last one. Bart told Jenkins the strange events began a few months ago. If there is a threat to pursue, it would make sense that the most current preempts the earlier volumes."

"Okay, I'll concentrate on that one," Alex replied and went to the keyboard to alter her program sequence.

The next morning, Jenkins drove up the driveway of Bart and Katherine's neighbor, Mark Griffin. Although his company, Griffin Enterprises, was headquartered in Florida, he spent most of his days in Bigfork and had a home office here. As Jenkins parked and walked to the door, he hoped his wife, Angie Griffin, was nowhere to be found.

Before he could touch the doorbell, however, the door opened, and she stood covered in sweat. She was breathing hard, and he could hear the TV blaring out dancing beat music and time intervals. He assumed she must be doing some kind of home video workout, and even without makeup, she looked amazing. Jenkins suspected she always did.

In a perky voice, she said, "Morning Sheriff, want to join me in a class?"

"Ah, no, ma'am, but thank you for the offer. I'm here to see your husband."

"Oh, he didn't mention it. Can you wait twenty minutes? I'll be done by then."

"Ms. Griffin, again I am here to speak with your husband. It is about Conrad Point Estates and initially, it is important I speak with him alone."

"Very well. His office is down the hall. The second door on the right. I'll be in once I'm done."

Jenkins simply nodded and walked to a set of double doors with the words Griffin Enterprises and its logo at eye level. Neither door had a window, so he knocked, expecting Griffin himself to answer. When the door swung open, an older woman in a business suit was standing in front of him.

"Good morning. You are Sheriff Jenkins?" she asked.

"Yes, ma'am. I'm here to see Mark Griffin."

"But of course. Please come in."

Jenkins entered in complete surprise. He had expected a room the size of a den or average office, but this was an entire wing of the house. No wonder it looked so big from the street.

She noted his surprise. "This is the Midwest office of Griffin Enterprises. We augment our headquarters in Florida. Please read and sign this," as she handed a wooden clipboard out to him.

He looked down at the clipboard with a handful of papers attached. "What is that?" he asked.

"Anyone entering this premise must sign an NDA with Griffin Enterprises and Mr. Griffin himself."

"Ma'am, I am here on a homicide investigation and don't much care about your rules and regulations. Please inform Mr. Griffin I'm here, or I'll send some folks over to bring him to my station."

She was clearly ready to confront him when a voice behind her said, "Claudine, it is all right. The Sheriff and I have some business to discuss."

She looked back at Jenkins coolly as Griffin placed his hand on Jenkins' shoulder.

"There are a lot of plans, photos, and items of interest here that are not public knowledge. The NDA protects us so we can work in the open."

Jenkins said nothing as they walked into his office, and the door closed. Griffin headed for one of two conversation chairs, and Jenkins took the second one.

"Nasty business with Bart. Good man. We were just getting started."

"You're referring to Conrad Point Estates?"

"Yes. Although we had several ideas in the works."

"Your wife has suggested Bart was having an affair. A short, cute gal that was hanging over him at your signing party at the Harbor Grill. Is that your conclusion as well?"

Griffin laughed. "Sheriff, my wife has become infatuated with crime stories. She says she's going to write a novel, which is fine, but her imagination is a bit unhinged. Bart was most certainly not having an affair."

"The girl?"

"A former employee. She was drunk and doesn't likely recall she was even trying to snag him. I fired her."

"Name?"

"Sally McBride. She lives in Kalispell."

"Did Bart ever mention his displeasure with Katherine?"

Griffin looked uncomfortable. "I'd rather not say Sheriff. I consider such discussions private."

"I understand, Mr. Griffin, but the man has been murdered, and the oldest motives in the world are money and infidelity."

Griffin shrugged. "Yes, of course. Listen, Bart loved his wife as a companion, but he wanted her to be more gregarious, more spontaneous. But she was none of those things. It bothered him, but he was highly unlikely to do anything about it."

"Why?"

"He was an old-fashioned romantic. Vows to him were sacred, so he wasn't happy, but stuck it out and had no intention of leaving Katherine or finding another woman."

"Katherine recalled Conrad Point Estate, but none of his other investments. Do you have any idea why Bart kept his business dealings away from her?"

"I was only aware of Conrad Point myself, but I'm surprised she didn't know of the other investments, considering their situation."

"Their situation?"

"Katherine is the one with the money. She financed his council seat and his senate runs and was also the money behind Conrad Point and, I can only imagine, any larger investments he might have had. She has millions."

"Good to know. Tell me about Conrad Point. Understand you had a lot of opposition."

"No more than normal. Investors and banks love development projects, but the people near them tend to feel left out. Add to that the views of the local tribal commission, and it was an uphill fight for close to six years."

"Which you resolved."

"Eventually. Our strategy is to maintain a strong legal team and ultimately wear them down before we bring the naysayers into the money. Works every time."

"You paid them off?"

"Not the way you're probably thinking. We created a special Conrad Point Estate tax, which is seven-tenths of one percent of the purchase price, payable to members of the newly formed Conrad Point Community Fund. That money, less administration fees, goes to the residents and tribes surrounding the project."

"How much does that work out to?"

"Around thirty-seven hundred dollars a year per household. We estimate the tax at nine hundred thousand net of expenses, and there are just under two hundred and fifty affected parties. Almost half are from the Confederated Salish and Kootenai Tribes of the Flathead Nation."

"Anybody think that wasn't enough?"

"No idea. We just broke ground, so any monies paid is still twelve months away."

"Mr. Griffin, in this and any project you were working on with Bart, can you recall any threats against him?"

"No. As a matter of fact, everyone loved him. I suspect you'll think less of me, but I brought Bart into Conrad Point because he was a friend of the Tribal Council. They respected him, and it was him, more than his money, that got us across the finish line."

"So, it is possible that someone who didn't want it could see him as the problem."

"I hadn't thought that, but crazy is crazy, right?"

The discussion went on for several more minutes when they concluded, and Griffin allowed him to use the employee entrance to avoid his wife. Jenkins considered talking to Katherine but decided to have Chase and his team research her background first.

Meanwhile, he headed to the address he had for one Sally McBride, which was a leased room over a bar in town. After several minutes with her, it was obvious the girl hardly recalled being there, and she was shocked to know he was a former senator who was now deceased. As he headed back to his SUV, he pulled out his pad and made a few notes. Although he had hoped for a quick win, it was clear this was going to take some time.

Chapter 8

Fortitude Security, Kalispell

The phone rang, and Richard picked up on the second ring. "Hey Billy, where are you? I have some news."

"Me too. I need you to dig into Katherine's past."

"Katherine Bartholomew?"

"Yes. According to Mark Griffin, she is the money behind Bart, and it was she who invested in Conrad Point Estates. They also had other projects planned, but when I asked her about the six million, she said they didn't have that kind of money. Since I'm close to this, I'll get Agent Stone to talk to her, but I want to arm him with the truth to see what she says."

"No problem. I'll get Alex on it right now."

"What do you have?"

"Alex ran her computer program against his hiking journal and got a hit. Seven months ago, Bart was hiking the Blackfoot Lake Trail in Jewel Basin and was off trail thinking he would try some fishing. He came across a small homeless campsite and described it as a few tents. Three weeks later, he returned to the same spot, but the encampment had grown to several tents and makeshift structures. He told the ranger about it, who said he was aware and was coordinating with other agencies to disband it. A week later, Bart was at the Misery Camp trailhead, and a guy jumped out of the bushes and said, '*Thanks a lot, you rich fucker. Someday, I'm gonna pay you back.*' Bart checked, and the ranger told him he was originally from Polson. His name is Fred Baker. Goes by Freddy."

"Oh shit. Everybody knows Freddy. Which journal was this in?"

"The most current. It starts on page thirteen."

"Okay. I'll run after him and see if anything pops up. Any luck on Conrad Point?"

"Still on it. We have seven individuals, including Griffin and Bartholomew, as well as two investment companies. One out of Florida does a lot with Griffin and one in Idaho. The others are making it tough to nail down."

"Okay, keep at it. I'm heading to the station."

That afternoon, Chase called Jenkins. "Any luck with the drifter?"

"Yes, and no. Baker is a local homeless guy with some obvious mental illness. Over the past six years, he has been arrested over twenty times in the towns around Flathead Lake. But it was always for vagrancy, public urination, or drunk and disorderly. No violence, no theft."

"Is he big enough to handle Bart's dead weight?"

"Hell no. The guy is in his sixties and weighs around one hundred and twenty-five pounds, soaking wet. Stone wants him pulled in regardless, based on his two-guy theory."

"Doesn't sound like a viable lead. Got time to hear about Katherine?"

"Sure."

"We have a rough profile on her that was easy to put together, so she's not hiding much. She was born in Whitefish to Hank and Rita Pullman. Her grandfather was Ulises Pullman. He made a fortune in Oil and Gas in Texas before moving to Whitefish. The Texas company was called Pullman Resources, which he sold in 1977 and is now part of a larger public company. The company he started in Montana was called Pullman Natural Resources (PNR), and it still exists. Katherine is not directly involved in the business, but her brother Larry is the CEO and is on the board of directors. The three surviving children of Hank and Rita are Larry, Matthew, and Katherine. The three control a trust that owns twenty-nine percent of the company. Those shares are worth over one hundred million at today's stock price."

"When did the parents die?"

"Rita in 1991, Hank in 1994," Chase replied as he read it from the fact sheet Alex had made for him.

Jenkins stated the obvious. "So, Katherine has a paper fortune of thirty-plus million."

"From PNR, yes, but each child also received six million in cash two years ago from the estate of the parents."

"Okay. Thanks for the fast turnaround. Stone is going to give her a run for her money. Since she appears to have lied to me, it's fair game."

"I'll keep the fire going for you if you need to blow off some steam later tonight."

"Yeah, do that," Jenkins said as he turned into the parking lot.

As he walked in, the door was only halfway open when Agent Stone barked off. "About time you showed up. Your deputies grabbed Baker, and he's getting cleaned up now. Let's wait for him."

"Lead the way," Jenkins said, keeping what he was really thinking to himself.

As they sat in the small interview room, Stone said, "I know you don't think he's good for it, but with help, he could have done this."

"Let's hear what he has to say," Jenkins replied.

Freddy Baker walked in and still smelled of smoke and other associated odors. He looked at Jenkins and said, "Hey, Sheriff Jenkins."

"Freddy," he replied before he got down to business.

"Freddy, your real name is Fred Baker, correct?"

"Yeah. You know that? Why are you asking?"

"Relax, Freddy, we're taping this conversation. For the record, I am Sheriff Billy Jenkins of Kalispell, Montana, station. With me is Special Agent Jeremy Stone with the Federal Bureau of Investigation."

"Feds! I ain't done nothing wrong," Baker snapped.

Jenkins ignored him. "Freddy, seven months ago, you lived in a tent encampment in Jewel Basin. Do you recall that?"

"Encampment? What's that?"

Stone jumped up. "Do not waste our fucking time. Answer the question."

Jenkins frowned and restated the question. "Freddy, did you live in a tent in Jewel Basin?"

"Yes sir, till we got thrown out," giving a look to Agent Stone.

"And how did you get thrown out?"

"Ranger Owens arrived with a bunch of guys and made us leave. Some horseshit about illegal structures, and we lacked the proper permits to stay there. It was pure bullshit, Billy. We weren't doing anything wrong."

"I understand. Shortly after, you approached a hiker at the Camp Misery trailhead. Do you recall that, Freddy?"

"Not really. I meet lots of hikers."

"Big guy. Says you threatened him."

"I didn't threaten anybody. I mean, look at me?"

"Freddy, you said, and I quote, "*Thanks a lot, you rich fucker. Someday, I'm gonna pay you back.*' Does that help you remember?"

"No, but it sounds like something I'd say." Baker smiled, but then frowned when Agent Stone nodded his head.

"Do you have a knife?"

"No. I used to, but I lost it. A big one," Baker replied as he held his hands a foot apart to show the size. Jenkins pushed the evidence photo of the knife in front of him.

"Look familiar?"

Excited, Freddy said, "Hell yeah. Can't believe you found it."

"So, this is your knife?"

"Oh, sure. I'd recognize that anywhere. What's that shit all over it?"

"Blood, human blood," Stone said bluntly.

Freddy looked over his hands and arms. "Never got a cut like that."

"Freddy, when was the last time you were at Swan River trail."

"Um, a few weeks ago."

"Trailhead or on the trail."

"Neither. I was living across the river."

"Where it flattens out after the thick brush?" Jenkins asked. Agent Stone was getting excited; you could see it on his face.

"Yeah, can't even walk through the brush. That's why it's a good spot."

"Do you own an ATV?"

"Nope."

"You sure?"

"Can't afford gas. What the heck would I do with it?"

"So, you were not on an ATV at your campsite on the opposite side of the river from Swan River Trail."

"No, sir."

"Did you see anyone who was?"

"No. I heard some when I was there."

"Heard but never saw?"

"That's right."

"Freddy, sit tight. Agent Stone and I need to discuss something." Jenkins stood up, and they both left.

When they were down the hall, Stone said what Jenkins assumed he would.

"How did you know of this man and the threat?"

"Bart said these odd events started a few months ago. I looked at his latest journal, and this entry was there. Freddy has been homeless for five or six years, and when I asked Owen Clark, the Ranger in Jewel Basin, if Freddy was there, he said yes."

"Why is this not in the file?"

"I only have time to update the file at night and haven't done it yet. I take it you think Freddy is a suspect."

"And you don't? He practically admitted to making the threat. He admitted it was his knife. He admitted he was at the crime scene and the point of the original threat. I'd say this man is toast."

"Freddy lacks the strength to push a ten-inch knife through a man's sternum who is almost a foot taller. Second, he could never get Bart onto an ATV, and third, if Bart bumped into him, it would not be as a friend. Last, he said he was there two weeks ago. We need to place him there two days ago."

"Then do it. This will wrap up nicely."

"Stone, this would be circumstantial at best. Baker is not going anywhere. Let's continue. I also need to bring you up to speed on Katherine Bartholomew. She lied to us."

"What about?" he said, alarmed, and Jenkins told him the story.

"So even you didn't know?"

"No. I've known the two of them since 1985 and never heard one word about her coming from money, although, to be fair, her dad died just four years ago."

"But if she has the money, it makes more sense if he had killed her. Not her killing him for using her money to make millions more."

"I don't think she killed him. But she knows more than she is saying and has already lied once."

"So, you'll bring her in?"

"Yes. I'd like you to question her at the Sheriff's station rather than here. She'll be more neutral. I'll have her here in an hour."

Chapter 9

Kalispell Sheriff's Station

It was over an hour later when a sleek Mercedes convertible with a dark blue cloth top and white leather interior pulled up to the sheriff's station. Behind the wheel was Angie Griffin and Katherine Bartholomew was in the passenger seat. They both entered.

Katherine saw the sheriff. "What is this about, Billy?"

"Afternoon Katherine. The FBI has some questions, and we thought it best if Ms. Griffin could get you out and past the reporters versus our arrival there. Shall we?" as he waved to his office before turning back to Angie.

"Ms. Griffin, you are welcome to wait or come back in, say, an hour."

"Come back? Nonsense, I need to be there with my friend. I'm sure the Agent Stone won't mind."

"And I can assure you he will. Stay here, please."

"Nope. Where she goes, I go, or we'll leave now."

Agent Stone walked out and looked at Katherine. "Ms. Bartholomew, I'm sorry for your loss and appreciate your voluntary cooperation. This way, please. Sheriff, see that Ms. Griffin is comfortable," and off they went.

Katherine turned, "Billy, I think you need to be there with me."

Jenkins knew what Agent Stone was trying to do. "I'm sorry, Katherine, but I have no choice but to make sure Ms. Griffin does not compromise this line of questioning."

Angie sat down in a huff and Billy sat down close to her. Stone had opened the door to Jenkins' office and allowed Katherine to enter before closing the door behind him.

"Mrs. Bartholomew . . ."

"Please call me Katherine."

"Very well, Katherine. When asked about the investment portfolio found in your husband's home office, you said that couldn't be true, stating you have money, but not that kind of money. Is that correct?"

"Yes. I said that to Sheriff Jenkins."

"But you inherited tens of millions of dollars. That is not something most people forget."

"I most certainly did not forget."

"But you said you didn't have that kind of money, although you really do. Why lie?"

"I didn't lie. I inherited the money, not Winston."

"So, are you saying your money is your money and his is his?"

"Not entirely, no. I have given him money over the years for his campaigns, and even the money for Conrad Point Estates, but all else is in a trust that only I control."

"But your husband was the beneficiary of the trust."

"He is not." Stone looked at her in disbelief.

"Agent Stone, that money is from my grandfather, Ulises Pullman. It can only be controlled by a Pullman, meaning if I die, my portion of the trust goes to my two brothers. If they die, their portion comes to me."

"Then how could you pull out millions? You just said you made the investment in Conrad Point."

"I can take out any sum over that which I initially inherited, but the original principal cannot be accessed, although I also inherited cash. Seriously, is this why you brought me here? I assumed your agency was more thorough in its investigation."

"Katherine, please. We had information suggesting you denied having money and another suggesting you have tens of millions. It was important to understand, which I now do. I'm not accusing you, just asking questions."

"Well, you could have fooled me," she said with a snarky voice.

"How much was invested in Conrad Point?"

"Three million."

"And what about the other three million?" He slid a piece of paper with a summary of each investment.

She didn't look, but replied, "I have no idea."

"I know this is a difficult time, but you seem to answer my questions while not revealing anything else. What is it you are not telling me?"

Without skipping a beat, she replied. "You mean that I am not impressed by you and assumed that my husband, a former Senator, would have commanded an agent of a much higher stature."

Stone didn't flinch. "Very good, Katherine. It is nice to see the real you come out to play." She smiled until he slammed his fist down onto the table, making her jump.

"What is it you're not saying?"

"Do you consider me a suspect, Agent Stone?"

"That's Special Agent Stone, and I don't suspect you as a murderer, but as an accomplice or accessory to murder, possibly. Polson Hardware. It's the third investment on the sheet you didn't even look at. You or your husband made close to a half-million dollar investment to add a small warehouse, feedstock, and rental center. You now own thirty percent of that business. How did that investment come about?"

"I know nothing about it. Other than our home, a first trust deed to a friend of approximately a half million, and the investment at Conrad Point. Polson Hardware means nothing to me. Who is the legal owner? Am I the beneficiary, or is it someone else?"

"We are still running down that information."

"So, rather than investigate, you thought it made more sense to strong-arm the widow of just forty-eight hours." She reached into her purse and withdrew a business card.

"All future inquiries can be done through my attorney. You'll find him very capable. No wonder you wouldn't allow Sheriff Jenkins in here. He'd have punched you in the nose, you rude bastard."

With that, she stormed out. Stone remained unphased, pleased he got her real character on tape. Wallflower? Loney wife? Bullshit.

After her hasty exit, both women left, and Jenkins joined Agent Stone to hear the tape of their conversation. Jenkins was not at all surprised that Stone had unnerved Katherine. But he was intrigued to learn what Stone meant by saying that he had gotten her to reveal her real self.

One thing the FBI is known for is criminal characterization and profiling. They employ thousands who can determine a person by their behavioral traits. Jenkins had known Katherine for over twenty years and honestly believed he had a firm picture of the woman, but now he questioned that.

Even Bart had made her out to be the weaker person's personality. But Katherine Bartholomew as the gatekeeper?

Jenkins, to his credit, did not react. He simply listened, and while it was no stretch to think Special Agent Stone could piss off a toilet seat, the last few lines of dialogue revealed a strong woman.

Jenkins spoke first. "Can she make trouble for you?"

"You mean, to go above me and say I hurt her feelings? Sure. It's happened before, and it will happen again. I don't give two shits about her. The only thing that matters is solving this murder, and I get results because I'm never too close."

"A bit cavalier, but I hear you."

"Grow a pair, Jenkins. You're a good cop. But you, my friend, are too close. Don't let that become a problem for me. So, what do you think?"

"We need to understand those investments."

"I'll give a list to my team; you do the same. Let's compare notes. What about Freddy Baker?"

"My advice is to let him go because he really won't go anywhere. If we need him, we can get him. You were able to establish that he wasn't there the night Bart was killed, so without evidence to tie him to the crime scene, he's not worth it."

"Still no additional evidence from the crime scene?" Stone asked.

"Nope. If it's there, Cheyenne will find it. The girl is a natural bloodhound."

Chapter 10

Fortitude Security, Kalispell, Day Three

Alex and Eddy had been working together to understand the investments under the fictitious name associated with Winston Bartholomew. To Chase, it was imperative they get behind this before Stone. It wasn't because he was competitive but because he wished to ward off the knee-jerk reactions Stone would arrive at without all the facts.

There were six investments outside of Conrad Point. Like Jenkins and Stone, Alex and Eddy knew all about Polson Hardware and Supply. The land and holdings were worth perhaps two million, and the business brought in almost thirty-five thousand in cash every month. Leveraged, that was worth a lot.

They also knew the Polson investment was made through an investment company called Capstone. That company was eventually traced to a company called Trinity Holdings in the Cayman Islands. It took Eddy twenty hours, but he eventually hacked into Trinity, and the company had three principals, none of whom were Winston "Bart" Bartholomew, or his wife. The transaction had been arranged by the law firm of Cartwright & Cartwright out of Florida and the attorney of record was Enrique Alvaro.

The next investment was a strip mall in Kansas. It was a quarter-million-dollar investment with an additional quarter-million-dollar construction loan, so presumably, they were fixing it up. The land and holdings were worth a million. On the property itself were five tenants, a laundromat, two bars, an unbranded 99-cent type store, and a private post-box office. They could not see the books because the owners had recently changed hands, but all stores were largely cash businesses. The investment company was called Newman Property Management, and it took Alex half the day to trace them to none other than Trinity Holdings. Cartwright & Cartwright had done the transaction, and similarly, the attorney of record was Enrique Alvaro.

The list continued. An apartment building in Whitefish; a capital investment project in Seattle and a construction company in New Jersey. Last was a small project in Detroit. They were all handled by a different investment company, but each one was linked to Trinity Holdings. And Cartwright & Cartwright handled all the transactions.

The only difference was the attorney of record. Enrique Alvaro handled three investments, and Alycia Gomes handled the remaining three.

Alex and Eddy had entered Chase's office and given him the update. He wheeled back his chair and stood, looking out the window at the lake in the rear of his property. He could see Nate riding one of the two rescued horses they stabled, Manny Vasquez was not far away, keeping a solid eye on him. Richard smiled as he turned back to them.

"Who are the three principals of Trinity Holdings again?"

Alex replied, "The first listed is Iyla Anderson. Next is Alan McDonald, and last is Logan Ellis. Each owns thirty percent. We're still trying to track them down."

"Who owns the remaining ten percent?" he asked.

"We haven't found it yet, but my guess is the law firm."

"Why?"

"Not sure, just seems to fit."

Chase nodded as though he understood and replied, "Keep digging, there has to be a tie to Bart or his wife. I'm going to go update Jenkins," as he walked away recalling Katherine's words, "*. . . mark my words, whatever is going on, it's much larger than my husband.*"

Chapter II

Cartwright & Cartwright, Miami, Florida

The weather in Florida was painfully humid after getting belted two weeks prior by tropical storm Mitch, the last major storm of 1998. Attorney Alycia Gomes rose from her desk and glanced around before she proceeded to the office of her college friend, Enrique Alvaro.

He glanced up as she walked in. "What's up?"

"I got an alert today from Trinity."

"What kind of alert?"

"IT group. Someone outside the firm accessed the Trinity files."

"Which files."

"Unknown."

"Okay, so what does that mean?"

"It means someone hacked into their system and opened one or more of our transactions."

"What makes you think they were our transactions?"

"Well, I guess I don't."

"Have you told Decco?" He was referring to their VP of Business Operations, Bernard Decco. He was not a partner since the Cartwright brothers would not allow any, but he was rumored to be their enforcer.

"No. What would I even say?" Alycia pleaded.

"Not sure, but if he finds out, it will look bad if we don't tell him."

"Jesus, what was I thinking coming here? I'm not a criminal."

"Alycia, all firms have bad clients. All firms go after money, don't be naïve."

"Do those firms supposedly have hit men on their payroll? Seriously, we have a nasty reputation."

"But we don't know that Alycia. There's no way?"

"Well, we seem to lose a lot of clients and staff," she countered.

"Listen, I'll tell him," he said, trying to help her.

"Thanks, Enrique, but I'll do it. I'm the one that talked to them, and they probably already called him."

He just nodded as Alycia headed out the door for the elevator. She entered, hit the twenty-eighth floor, and waited for the door to close before she finally let out a breath.

When it opened, she froze. Standing there waiting for the elevator was none other than Bernard Decco. They made eye contact.

"Alycia, were you coming to see me?"

"Yes, I need to talk to you," she replied nervously.

"Very well."

He turned and headed to his office as he said casually with a smile, "And here I was, coming to you."

She followed him, thankful she had come to him.

Chapter 12
Kalispell Sheriff's Station

Jenkins was having coffee when Stone entered, and he started to say something when his phone rang. He held up his finger to Jenkins to say *hold on* and walked to the opposite corner of the small station. The acoustics made it easy to hear the one-sided conversation that Stone would soon wish he had taken outside despite the cold weather.

Jenkins heard Stone saying, "I understand, sir, but your facts are incorrect."

"Well, no, I'm not saying your intel is wrong. It's just that she mischaracterized the exchange. She is hiding something, and I was able to get her to break."

"No, I didn't get new information, but I got her to show that she is not the shrinking violet she has everyone believing."

"Yes, I know who she is ..."

"Of course, I'll respect her as a widow, but she is involved. I just don't yet have proof. But I'll get it."

"I understand."

"I said, I understand. Thank you, sir."

And he hung up. Once the call was disconnected, he sighed, and for a second, Jenkins thought he was going to throw the phone through the window. Standing straight, he adjusted his tie and walked into Jenkins' office. Thankfully, Billy had wiped the smile off his face in time.

"You probably loved that."

"Morning Stone. Loved what?"

"My call."

"I'm sorry?" Jenkins said, acting dumb, as he looked over at his coffee pot and asked, "Want a cup?"

"No thanks. I don't do stimulants."

"It's coffee, not speed."

"Caffeine is highly addictive."

"Suit yourself, any news?"

"No. You?"

"Nothing yet. Whoever we are dealing with is not an amateur," Jenkins said, knowing he was merely stating the obvious.

Stone replied, "We traced two investments to out-of-state investment companies, but they don't appear to be legitimate."

"That can't be a complete surprise. But I suspect we'll have those answers soon. Then what. Do we arrest Katherine and pressure her into getting a name?"

"Until three minutes ago, that is exactly what I would have done, but the poor little widow called the Director of the FBI. She called the fucking Director! Who even has that number?" Stone yelled before calming himself.

"She was miffed about yesterday?" Jenkins asked.

"Yes, sheriff, she was miffed and explained it in a way only a woman could, and my boss just blew her exact words straight up my ass."

"But this is your thing, right?"

"Yeah, of course. But we need results soon. Very soon," Stone said, unsure of himself, as he turned and left the building.

The email on Jenkins' computer beeped an hour later, and there was new information from Chase. Apparently, the kids had some information, and Jenkins printed it off, memorized the salient points, and headed down the street to the FBI office. Stone needed to see this.

After meeting with him privately and describing the details, he handed him a synopsis for the file. Stone asked outright. "Where did this information come from?"

"My team. I have some young kids in town who get computers and really understand search engines. It's not all admissible, but it leads to intelligence, that is."

"It's that smartass cowboy, right?"

"Doesn't matter, Stone. All investment firms used are fake, and all end up at Trinity Holdings in the Caymans. All transactions were handled by the same law firm, and we have the names of both lawyers involved. I think you can put your team on a fishing expedition," Jenkins replied with some authority.

"Where would you start?" Stone asked uncharacteristically.

"Have your team dig into the law firm. Meanwhile, let's go back to Mark Griffin. His Florida headquarters is just a mile from the offices of Cartwright & Cartwright," as he grabbed his hat and left for his truck with Stone right behind him.

They talked little as they drove to the Griffin's home office, and Jenkins wondered if Stone was on board with Chase. While Jeremy Stone appeared an asshole on first meeting him, so could Richard Chase.

But Jenkins knew what others didn't. Richard Chase was a flawed man trying to make himself better. Despite his prick of a father, his asshole brothers, and losing his mom and sister, he never used any of that to define him. Instead, Chase used those experiences to change into something better.

Compared to most people Jenkins had to deal with, that was a rarity. Most, with a similar upbringing, only became narcissistic, blaming everyone else for their problems. But not Richard Chase. He took everything smack on the chin and then tried to learn from it. And if that wasn't the definition of character, what was?

Sure, Stone could not embrace some of Fortitude's methods, but it was a path forward, even if it was in the background.

He had called ahead. As they walked along the stone walkway to the front door, Mark Griffin came around from the back of the house.

"Morning Sheriff. And you would be Special Agent Stone, I take it?"

"Yes," Stone said sharply.

"Nice to meet you, I'm Mark Griffin. Let's walk around to the back."

"No office today?" Jenkins asked.

Griffin replied, as he smiled, "Presence of law enforcement day after day makes the troops nervous."

"Why? Are they doing something that might interest us?" Stone asked coldly.

Griffin glanced at Stone but said nothing as they sat. He offered them coffee or tea, but neither were takers and Stone elected to ramp up the heat.

"We are here regarding investments by Winston Bartholomew. You were his financial advisor?"

"Not at all, Agent Stone. I'm a developer, not a banker."

Stone continued. "But you know of his investments?"

"No, I don't. He and I were only involved in Conrad Point. I am not aware of any investments made based on conversations we had together."

"But yet you're aware of his investment portfolio?" Stone replied with a smirk.

"Only because Sheriff Jenkins told me so yesterday. So, yes, I am aware he had other investments, but I did not steer him to them."

Jenkins asked. "Did you frequent Bart's man cave on the side of the house?"

"Sure, we all did. Bart had an exceptional taste in spirits, so it would make little sense to pass the opportunity if you liked to drink and smoke cigars."

"So, the term 'we' is like neighbors, friends from Bigfork?" Jenkins asked.

"Yes, and occasionally, friends of mine."

"Investment friends?"

"Yes, although we rarely talked business. This was always a social gathering."

"Anyone from a law firm one block from your headquarters in Florida, perhaps? Cartwright & Cartwright?" Stone asked to get a reaction.

Although Griffin tried to stop it, the name provoked a reaction. As he caught his expression, he tried to speak, but the words didn't come out at first. He cleared his dry throat, coughed, and then tried again.

"I know of them, but no."

"Does Griffin Enterprises use their services?"

"No."

"So, they are a firm you personally use?"

"I simply know of them, Agent Stone. What is your point?"

"We think there is a relationship between Bartholomew's investments and this firm. Given their proximity to your company, I just wondered if you also used them. But fine, you know them. How?"

"They advertise in publications I frequent, and I have discussed certain concepts with them but found their costs exceeded our budget by a wide margin."

Stone then went deeper. "So, Conrad Point almost used Cartwright?"

"No project of Griffin Enterprises has used the firm, Agent Stone."

"So, it was a personal investment?"

Griffin answered, although it was clear he was losing his patience. "I rarely make them. My business keeps me working twelve hours a day, and I honestly don't need more money."

"What about the Cayman Islands? Does Griffin Enterprises use that locale as a method of tax avoidance?"

"We deploy a variety of legal means to reduce taxation."

"In the Caymans?" Stone badgered him again.

"I've already answered the question, Agent Stone."

He reached into his shirt pocket, a shirt that neither Jenkins nor Stone could afford, and withdrew the card of another attorney out of Miami, Florida.

"I have a sense for your line of questioning, and while I don't understand how my neighbors' investments are related to me, you clearly think they are. I invite you to work through my attorney from this point forward. If that is all?"

And he stood as if to end the meeting.

"Mr. Griffin, if you have plans to travel, please let us know. I suspect we will have more questions for you."

"And once you have provided those questions to my attorney, and we have reviewed them, I will gladly make myself available. Until then, I'm free to do whatever I wish. I'm sure you can find your way back to the front."

Griffin made for the house as his wife, Angie, looked down on them from the second floor. When Jenkins made eye contact with her, she smiled and walked out of view.

Stone looked at Jenkins as they headed to the front of the expansive lawn, heading for his truck. "Well, we have him sweating a bit."

"Yeah, the guy went from super cooperative to shut down mode in the span of twenty-four hours."

Stone turned to him and said seriously, "Sounds like this Cartwright & Cartwright is no ordinary law firm."

Attorney Enrique Alvaro finished his workout and after a shower and getting dressed, he stopped at a Starbucks around the corner. Waiting for the barista, she finally asked for his order, which he gave her. A grande Americano with three shots of espresso.

As he stepped back, a woman approached him from behind without him taking notice.

"What can you tell me about the investments you made for Winston Bartholomew through Trinity Holdings?" she asked.

Alvaro froze. Despite the air conditioning on high, he started to sweat when the woman added, "It was not a complex question."

"Who are you?" Alvaro said without turning to face her.

"FBI, You're running out of time, Enrique."

"I have no idea what you are talking about. I don't know anything about a company called Trinity Holdings, or a man named Bartholomew."

"I have documents that say otherwise."

"As an attorney in a pool of paralegals and others, my signature can be used for certain filings."

The barista shouted, "Enrique," as he stepped forward to get his coffee. Turning toward her now, he said to the woman, "Sorry I could not help you further."

"You're making a big mistake, Mr. Alvarez."

"So are you," he warned as he walked out.

Agent Veronica Williamson held her own coffee and then stepped outside to call Special Agent Stone, who answered immediately.

"What do you have?"

"Last night, I confronted Alycia Gomes at a restaurant, and I just met Alvarez. Both said virtually the same thing that their signatures can be used by the firm for certain filings, and they know nothing about Trinity Holdings or the Senator."

"A scripted response?" Stone asked.

"Absolutely."

"Who is the weaker of the two?"

"Gomes, without a doubt. Alvarez was nervous but quickly pulled it together. She is in way over her head."

"Let them fester and then confront Gomes again. With a backup agent, bring her into the downtown office and offer her immunity for information."

"Done."

Chapter 13

Griffin residence, Bigfork

Mark Griffin walked from the rear yard and headed straight to his office, closing his door as he entered despite three people vying for his time. It was too early for a drink, so he focused his breathing, hoping to lower the anxiety that had built up in his mind. He was not at all worried about the FBI or the local sheriff, but he was very worried about Cartwright & Cartwright.

He knew of them alright. But had Winston Bartholomew invested in them? Clearly, the FBI believed he had. Griffin found that hard to believe since the former senator was once part of a special commission that had once investigated the law firm. The whole affair had been dubbed the "Keating Five" when the Senate investigated five of their own in the late 1980s.

The investigation involved the senators and Lincoln Savings and Loan Association. The five had been urged by the owner, Charles Keating, to convince the Federal Home Loan Bank Board not to investigate the firm's risky investments. They did, and the board backed off, only for Lincoln to collapse a year later. The result was a taxpayer bailout of over three billion dollars and the beginning of a massive banking collapse that followed. As it turned out, Keating had donated over a million dollars to the campaigns of the same five Senators.

It was during that investigation that Cartwright & Cartwright was briefly in the crosshairs of the US Senate. They were one of the law firms that handled several of Lincoln's larger risky investments.

The law firm itself was owned by brothers William and Randle Cartwright, who were subsequently fined by Florida banking regulators, but they admitted no wrongdoing.

Griffin's concern was that with Bartholomew dead, Cartwright would learn he was being questioned, and they tended to act first and ask questions later. He even began to think they may have even killed the former senator. If true, they would not hesitate to kill him if they thought he would sell them out.

It was a calculated risk, but it made sense to get himself off the hook by alerting them to the FBI's questioning.

The call took place later that day. The contact he had was most certainly not the Cartwright brothers. Instead, it was their head of Business Operations, Bernard Decco.

Griffin had never met him but knew of him as the phone rang. He was using a prepaid or burner phone because it was untraceable, but Decco would know the number and soon answered.

"Trouble in paradise?" Decco asked.

"Perhaps Mr. Decco. The FBI and a local sheriff are asking about Cartwright, and specifically, investments made by Winston Bartholomew. He was recently murdered."

"I am aware. Give me the specifics of their inquiry."

Griffin did. "What should I do."

"Do nothing, Mr. Griffin. His investments are not yours, but I appreciate the heads-up. Do you require any assistance?"

Griffin, unsure of the question, said, "No, this is nothing to be concerned about for me, but you needed to know they have a bead on your firm."

"As does everyone else. Thanks." And the phone went silent. Griffin hung up, hoping that was enough to keep him alive. He also noted that Decco said *his investments are not yours.* Bart had invested with them.

In nearby Kalispell, Richard sat in a conference room with Alex and Eddy. The topic was the law firm of Cartwright & Cartwright. "So, what do we have?"

Alex spoke first. "On the surface, they are a family-owned firm with excellent credentials. Once tied to a scandal, they rebranded after a modest fine but never changed how they make their money. They create dummy corporations for a fee and do it very well. They are also known for elaborate money and anti-taxation schemes for the uber-rich."

"Anything else?"

"On the dark web, there is a lot of chatter regarding their ability to make problems disappear, which are said to include clients, witnesses, and employees."

"Are you saying disappear like murder?"

"Unknown but suspected."

"Who is their enforcer?"

"The dark web has several threads that include the name Bernard Decco. He passed the bar in 1985 but does not seem to involve himself in cases. The last one he was on record for was 1987, so close to eleven years ago. Cartwright is weird in that the two brothers, William and Randle, will not allow the firm to hold other partners. As a result, they pay their top attorneys very well, and Decco appears to be part of the inner circle."

"Meaning what?"

"The sum of the dark web paints him as managing their 'problems,' so we think he's a fixer."

"And by fixer, you mean threats, extortion, and possibly murder?" Richard asked.

"Yes. Specifically, he takes care of enemies and problems that could cause trouble for the firm," Eddy replied.

Richard gave that a thought. "I have to say, it seems impossible that a company can simply kill anyone that is a threat to them. But I guess that is a question of frequency. An occasional death might go uncovered. But if it happens with regularity, it would be hard to hide."

Alex chimed in. "There is no specific proof here until we dig into the leads we have. It's just people talking and thinking that nobody knows what they said. A legitimate legal business is what they want everyone to see, but the real money comes primarily from helping people hide money and escape taxes behind these false fronts. Occasionally, they must meet some resistance."

"Why would there be resistance from paying clients?"

"Divorce, prosecution deals, remorse, who knows? I'm only saying the dark web knows them as a firm whose threats often disappear. The implication is that if you deal with them, you accept the consequences. But if you go after them, they play for keeps."

"And if Cartwright, who has a habit of removing problem clients, is behind Bart's investments, perhaps they killed him?" Richard said, thinking out loud.

"Nothing includes the name Winston or Katherine Bartholomew, or Mark Griffin," Eddy replied.

"Do you think they know you have penetrated their systems?"

"Probably. We would appear as Russian hackers if they're good. Hard to say if they could pierce the veil we have created," Alex said with confidence.

"Back off and see what they do."

Richard knew little about computers, but the kids had given him enough of a crash course that he knew some of their tricks.

He left them and went to his office to make a call he had been regretting. A call to Crime Scene Investigator, Cheyenne Denton.

Despite Cheyenne's desire, Richard was still a married man. He had met his wife, Darna Bautista Chase, in Cavite City, Philippines, when he was on assignment there as a Navy SEAL. Although reluctant to have any relationship, given his career and lifestyle, he was attracted to her, and they started to date. Soon, they were living together between missions and eventually married. A year later, they had their son Nate, who was now eleven.

After Richard's discharge, Nate and Richard returned to the United States while Darna remained in the Philippines. They still cared for each other and met occasionally.

But the truth was Darna, a scientist with the Petron Corporation, hated violence and the fear that could arise from it. At one time, she tolerated what Richard did because he was a soldier for his government. But when he started Fortitude and essentially put himself in harm's way for money, she started to have a problem with his profession.

It was on a potentially massive case for Fortitude just a year after the company started when a disgruntled client kidnapped Nate. Even though Richard and Billy got him back unharmed and arrested the kidnappers, it was the last straw for Darna.

So, while they weren't together, they kept up appearances for their son, who had always known them to be apart. But he also knew they were very much his mom and dad.

It was in another Fortitude case last year when Richard met Cheyenne, who had transferred from Missoula to Kalispell at around the same time. Like Darna, Cheyenne's personality reminded him of his sister, Mary Anne, who he had loved dearly. She had overdosed when she was twenty-three, and Richard had hunted down the drug dealer who killed her with his tainted drugs. It was righting that wrong that made him want to help others, which created Fortitude.

But unlike Darna, Cheyenne was a CSI, unaffected by the rough stuff. That she acted like a tomboy put Richard at ease. Although he never intended it, she had interrupted his willingness to hang out with her and talk shop as he was into her.

One night out by his lake, they had been drinking a bit after a tough day, and Cheyenne took advantage of the situation. Richard didn't stop it, and although nothing really happened, it was clear they had feelings for one another. The passion was real and explosive, but his conscience got the better of him, and he stopped before it went too far. But it ate at him he had even allowed it to happen. He had avoided her in all but work-related meetings ever since.

He had never told Darna and probably never would, but these feelings were a reminder to him they had to solve whatever had happened between them or consider moving on.

The phone rang several times, but Cheyenne didn't pick up, so he would call again.

It was just past seven when she called him back.

"Sorry, Richard. We've been at the crime scene all day." She was referring to the area where Bart had been found as she led a team of three, trying to locate his gun and any blood residue.

"Any luck?" he asked.

"Yes. One of my team just took the evidence to the Forensic Science Division in Missoula. Listen, I haven't called Dr. Kingman, Sheriff Jenkins, or Agent Stone, so this is between us, okay?"

While Dr. Kingman was the coroner for Kalispell, Missoula had superior forensic capabilities, and Stone demanded that evidence be compiled there.

"Understood," Chase said without question.

"We found the gun and two blood samples. I'll need them tested to understand what it means. Based on the large blood sample, this was the actual crime scene. The second sample is small but may provide trace DNA from the killer."

"Enough blood to matter?"

"Not nearly enough to incapacitate the killer, but enough to pull DNA."

"Stone is convinced we have two perps," Chase added.

"Yeah, I heard that from Kingman, but there's no evidence to support that. So, how are you?"

"Okay, I guess. Working behind the scenes is not my style, but Billy has it worse with Special Agent Stone."

"Billy can handle him. I miss talking to you."

"Listen, I enjoy talking to you too, but ..."

"But what, soldier boy?"

He hated that expression, but let it go. "Cheyenne, I like you, but I'm not available and don't know if I ever will be."

"I know I'm pushy, but you're a guy worth fighting for. And I get your situation, but you two haven't been together, together in what, like, five years."

"I know that, but Darna is still Nate's mom, and she's still my wife until she's not. Right now, she is."

"Okay, sorry, I'm not trying to make you feel bad. I just like you, and it seemed for a while you liked me, too."

"I did ... and still do. I just can't act on it."

She noted his voice rise and decided not to push further. "Fine, but I won't wait forever. Just saying."

Chapter 14

FBI Resident Agency Kalispell

"Thanks, Dr. Kingman," Stone said as he hung up the phone. He glanced toward Jenkins. "Your CSI found two traces of blood and the gun and sent the samples to the forensics lab in Missoula. Kingman just confirmed the large sample matches the victim and shows his place of death. The second sample is that of the suspected killer, and it included some gunshot residue, so he or she was wounded by Bartholomew's gun."

"Did the weapon hold Bart's fingerprints?"

Stone nodded. "Yes. They are sending ballistic information as well as the electropherograms of both DNA samples."

"But no DNA matches?"

Stone shook his head no. "Nothing in the Montana DNA Identification Index or the National DNA Database for the killer. The DNA for Bartholomew matches 100 percent."

Jenkins said gruffly, "God forbid we get a break. How much distance was between the crime scene and where his body was dumped?"

Stone replied without his normal smartass attitude. "That's the weird part. Less than a hundred feet. The CSI team assumed that given the suspected ATV tracks, they would start the search a thousand feet out and then work their way in."

"Odd indeed. The killer confronts Bart almost as soon as he crossed the river, kills him, and then drops the body less than a house length away. Perhaps the body fell off the ATV?"

"So, the killer intended to take the body farther away but got stuck. When the body falls off, he panics and flees the scene."

"Let's talk to Cheyenne, we need to firm that up," and Jenkins dialed her number.

She answered. "Sheriff Jenkins, what's up."

"Cheyenne, I'm here with Agent Stone. Previously, we discussed the odd body position at the original crime scene, and today, we know he was killed at another location. But the two crime scenes are close together, making us wonder why the killer might have used an ATV."

"Okay, following you so far, go on," she replied.

"We think the killer tried to carry away the body, intending to take it much further away, but got stuck in the mud. Once that happened, he or she then tried to break free, and in the process, Bart's body fell off the back. Is there any evidence to support that?"

"From the blood location to the dump site, the ATV tire depth in the soft ground goes from one to seven inches. At the dump site, it suddenly goes to fourteen inches and gradually reduces back to hard ground, so yes, that fits. That deeper trough is consistent with spinning the tires and getting bogged down. With the weight off the back, the killer could get free."

"Okay, thanks," Jenkins said as he hung up, not sure if this was relevant.

Back at Fortitude, Eddy Laughlin swept his fingertips over his keyboard. There, he followed thread after thread into the possible identity of the three principals of Trinity Holdings.

The Cayman Islands are considered a tax haven because they do not impose taxes on residents or businesses domiciled there. That means no income taxes, property taxes, capital gains taxes, payroll taxes, or withholding tax. It is a perfect place for a corporation from a high tax country to establish an offshore subsidiary and direct all profits there rather than the parent company. The shell corporation is then subject to the tax laws of the Cayman Islands rather than say, the United States.

Trinity Holdings was not a corporation, but rather an LLC governing hundreds of investments by rich people all over the world. Apparently, people like Winston Bartholomew and possibly his neighbor, Mark Griffin.

Alex had hacked into them and uncovered the names of the three principals, who each owned thirty percent. What Eddy was doing was trying to determine who they really were.

It had been almost twenty hours since he started, and he found that each of these names was related to a deceased individual. Iyla Anderson was a widow from San Francisco in California who was murdered in 1980; the case was still unsolved. Alan McDonald was from Scotland and passed away in 1966. The last, Logan Ellis, was from the United Kingdom and died in 1978.

Eddy was now trying to determine the heirs. Someone was collecting the profits from Trinity, but it wasn't one of the deceased. He was also looking at who owned the last ten percent.

Alex had theorized that Cartwright & Cartwright owned this and was thus compensated for the business they steered to Trinity. But Eddy could not find a single name that had any relation to the law firm and certainly not the two owners, William or Randle Cartwright.

It was an hour later when he got a hit. He checked, double checked, and then headed for Richard's office.

Eddy walked into his office and sat down. It wasn't often Eddy came to the boss because, while he respected Chase immensely, he also feared him. Seriously, this was a guy who knew how to kill people. In Eddy's geek world, that made him a real-life character from one of his video games.

"Eddy, what's up?" Richard asked.

Eddy explained the names were related to dead people and did not seem to have any connection via their spouses or families, although he was still working on that. In the search for the minor share partner, he had a name.

"Who is it?

"Matthew Pullman."

Richard looked at him in surprise. "As in, the brother of Katherine Bartholomew?"

"Yes. I checked and double-checked."

"Nice work, Eddy. I'm not sure what it means, but this would all make perfect sense if Katherine was involved with Cartwright & Cartwright," Chase replied, knowing what he was saying.

Eddy left, and Richard phoned Billy Jenkins, who immediately phoned Agent Stone. An hour later, they were back at the Bartholomew residence.

"Sheriff Jenkins, I wasn't aware you were coming over," Katherine said. "I'm afraid I'm not prepared for guests."

Agent Stone had taken a call. When he walked up and stood next to Jenkins, Katherine sighed and asked, "Why is he here?"

Jenkins said straight out. "We have some additional questions, Katherine. Can we come in? It is best the reporters don't try to interpret our conversation."

"Must I allow him?" she said to Jenkins.

Before Jenkins could say anything, Stone barked. "I'm running this investigation. If you would prefer, we can drive back to the FBI station. It's your call."

She allowed them in. To Agent Stone, she said coldly, "What is it I have done now."

"You tell me?"

Disgusted, she barked, "You're a bully. What do you want?"

"When did you last speak to your brother, Matthew?" Stone asked.

"Matthew? What does he have to do with anything?"

"It was a simple question, Katherine."

"We haven't spoken in months, although he and my older brother have tried to reach me. I assume they heard about Bart, but I just don't wish to talk to them."

"Why?"

"Because they are assholes, Special Agent Stone. We own and manage the Pullman trust equally, but they have always acted as though they run it, and I'm just along for the ride. The stupid girl."

"Mrs. Bartholomew, the six investments that your husband was involved with all used the same law firm. The investments are funneled through a single shell company in the Caymans, and it appears your brother is a financial participant in that company."

"That is not possible. Larry is the smart one. Matthew fancies himself as a successful playboy, but I assure you, he has limited business insight and isn't capable of complex tax avoidance scenarios."

"You seemed to understand the subject?"

"I do not. I'm merely articulate."

"Very well. Do you have an address for your brother?"

"Yes, Larry lives in Whitefish, and Matthew lives in New York. Let me get the address."

She pulled up her phone and sent Jenkins the information on each.

"So, you are going to question him?" she asked.

"Most likely. I would appreciate it if you did not warn him in advance," Stone said, mindful of his words.

"Why would I do that? I have established that I dislike him." She paused and then added, "Billy, you don't think Matthew had something to do with Bart's murder."

"I have no idea, Katherine. We just need to follow this lead, since it might be related to Bart's investments."

"He's broke, you know. His wealth is only on paper."

"Who? Matthew?"

"Yes, he has always spent more than he makes. For years, Larry gave him additional funds until he finally wised up. That made Matthew run to me, but I turned him down immediately, so he left me alone."

"When was the last time Larry gave him money?"

"Perhaps six months. You would have to ask him," she replied.

"We will."

An hour later, Stone and Jenkins headed directly for the Glacier International Airport where they took the FBI jet to New York. They needed to locate Matthew Pullman.

If Pullman was having financial problems, it wasn't obvious from the large Brownstone that graced Jane Street near Greenwich as they drove up. The four-story property with a garden off the second floor had been built a hundred years before and was worth several million dollars, possibly more. They exited their staff car, which was double parked, its blue lights blinking on and off, and headed up the steps to the door. Agent Stone knocked.

There was no answer and when Stone knocked again, Jenkins peered through the upper pane of the glass topped door.

"Stone, you need to call for backup. We have a body."

Inside, a woman was lying on the floor in a pool of blood. Stone called in a request for backup, knowing it would likely come from NYPD.

They arrived within ten minutes, and Stone introduced himself and Jenkins. Two NYPD patrols were present, and they removed their service weapons. Stone approached the door. When he tried the handle, he was surprised to find it unlocked.

With his foot, he pushed the door open slightly and said loudly, "Matthew Pullman. FBI."

Nothing, not a sound.

They entered and walked toward the body of the woman. Stone approached her and noted the single gunshot to her forehead. Rather than use the elevator, they started for the stairs in defensive positions. The NYPD officer inside with them called in the body and requested more backup as the second officer protected the entrance.

Outside, neighbors had gathered.

On the stairs, walking slowly, their guns were out, but it was obvious in the first few steps they were too late. Blood leaves a metallic smell in the early hours of a crime scene, but it is soon overpowered by the natural smells of death. From the body's natural release of fluids to decay, the odor was unmistakable.

They followed the stairs to the study, where their suspicions were confirmed. Matthew Pullman was strapped to a leather wing chair. His feet and hands were bound, and whoever the killer might have been, they didn't just kill him. They slowly cut him in strategic places until he bled to death. His hollow face and body were terrifying in appearance, as was the handkerchief still in his mouth, the chair surrounded by significant pools of fresh and dried blood.

Someone had taught Matthew Pullman a lesson. Why?

Chapter 15

Midtown, Manhattan, New York

After hours of discussion with the FBI's New York field office and the NYPD, Stone and Jenkins were finally able to return to Kalispell. The murder of Pullman and his maid was bizarre and unexpected for the posh neighborhood, although neighbors saw nothing and heard nothing. CSI teams were combing the 6,000-square-foot home for clues, and early thoughts suggested a mid-to-late afternoon attack. The maid had been cooking, and Pullman had been surprised in his own home office.

As they reentered the station close to ten in the evening, Jenkins said to Stone. "So, do you ever wind down?"

"Not following Jenkins."

"I usually head over to Chase's cabin and have a glass of something. Any interest?"

"Not much of a drinker."

"Okay, suit yourself." Jenkins grabbed his hat and started out.

"Do you think he'd be offended if I tag along?" Stone asked, noting Jenkins' surprise.

Jenkins smiled. "It's not a problem. He's a lot like you. You really can't offend him."

As he drove, Jenkins began to wonder if that was true since it was Stone after all, but he had never seen Chase hold a grudge over personalities.

He pulled into the circular drive of decomposed granite and stopped the truck. They went in without knocking, and Jenkins made himself a scotch and grabbed a beer for Stone. They went out to the patio, where they found Richard looking at the fire.

He turned at the sound and said, "Evening, guys. Pull up by the fire. It's cooling off."

They did, and Jenkins filled Chase in on the deaths in New York. Stone figured it was the Fortitude bunch that likely made the connection between Pullman and Trinity Holdings.

At first Chase said nothing, but then asked, "Was it true he was having financial problems?"

Stone answered. "Yes. Three million in late payments and taxes. Default judgement was filed two months ago. I take it you made the connection?"

"One of my analysts did."

"I thought I clarified you were to stay out of this."

"You did, but Fortitude has been hired by Katherine Bartholomew. We're trying hard not to step on any toes but provide directional intel."

"She only hired you to make her look innocent. Not sure where this leaves us, but one thing is clear: we're making somebody nervous, which means we're getting close." Chase and Jenkins both nodded.

"But we don't have the key that holds this together. Bart somehow uses Katherine's money to make high pay-out investments through Cartwright & Cartwright. It is also possible he did this through Matthew Pullman, not Mark Griffin, as was initially suspected. Pullman, however, is broke, and both brother and sister refused to give him a lifeline. How does that tie into the murder of Bartholomew?" Chase replied.

Jenkins took a slight pull on his drink. "Maybe Pullman, who needs money, brought in Bart to make a healthy commission."

Stone pondered the thought and said, "Pullman needed much more than ten percent of what, three million? I didn't know Bartholomew, but I suspect he didn't do this for the investments. I think he finds out that Pullman is connected, and both he and his wife realize her brother is in with the wrong crowd. Maybe the 'investments' were only created to get the dirt necessary to expose them?"

"And Cartwright finds out the former Senator is behind the investments and attempts to scare Bart before they kill him. Making us think it was a local matter," Chase said with interest.

"That works, but then why kill Pullman?" Jenkins asked.

"Perhaps they knew we were on our way to question him," Stone asked.

Chase replied, "Doubtful, given the personal nature of the killing. I still think Bart knew his killer, so perhaps it was Matthew Pullman. It's been three days since the murder, so not much of a problem to get back to New York after killing him."

Stone replied, "We'll check flights and private wings out of Glacier Airport. But why would Pullman help Bartholomew with the investments if the purpose was to get intel on Trinity and, or Cartwright & Cartwright? Pullman was making serious money off Trinity, and besides, there was no way Cartwright allowed Bartholomew in. He's the enemy."

Jenkins replied, "Maybe Pullman exposes Bart to save his own skin, not realizing they already knew it was him who brought him in. They make Pullman kill Bart to save his own skin and then kill Pullman, anyway."

"Sounds like something they would do, but I'm with Stone; why would Pullman even bring him in? He knows how the firm operates. That's suicide," Chase replied.

Stone took a sip of his beer, which just made him colder, although he would never admit it. Seriously, who sits outside drinking an ice-cold beverage when the ambient temperature is fifteen frigging degrees. Shit, if he didn't drink this fast, it was going to freeze.

"We're looking deeper into his finances, but we need to wrap this up. My boss is concerned about the body count, and the enforcers for Cartwright & Cartwright appear to be cleaning up based on our moves. How the hell do they follow what we're thinking?"

"We've held this pretty close to the vest," Jenkins said defensively.

Stone nodded and said, “I say we get a warrant for the phone records of Mark Griffin and Katherine Bartholomew. See if either has called Florida or the Cayman Islands.”

Jenkins and Chase nodded.

Chapter 16

Forensic Science Division Substation, Missoula

Eighty miles away, two men sat in an idling car, momentarily taking advantage of the car's heater behind a large stone building. Like many in Montana, most State and Federal buildings were Greek neoclassical in style, and this building for the Montana Department of Justice was no exception. After ten minutes, they exited and went around the perimeter. It wasn't for exercise, but rather to avoid the exterior cameras they had observed.

Dressed in black with blacked out faces, they proceeded to the rear. There, they climbed up the outside of the building using a large downspout from the roof rain gutter system. That corner of the building was in camera view but ostensibly dark as the spotlight on the front facade made this area pitch-black. A shadow in the nighttime.

They entered the second floor, and again avoided cameras as they descended to the basement. In areas where the cameras were placed, they shut off the lights in the hallway as they made their way down to the morgue. There, they observed the interior through a small window. A vestibule allowed the room to be isolated from the hallway environment, and although they could see no one, someone was there.

The first figure entered without a sound and switched off the lights. A minute later, his partner came in and closed the primary door.

Inside her small office, Lab Technician Roxy Le Blanc sat with Cheyenne Denton. They were so focused on her screen that neither noticed the lights behind them had just gone out, although Cheyenne noticed the screen suddenly seemed darker.

"What was that?" Cheyenne asked.

"What was what?" Roxy said as she blinked her eyes, knowing she was getting tired.

"The monitor just dimmed."

"I'm honestly too tired to notice."

Cheyenne turned and saw the morgue lights behind her had gone out. "The lights just turned off. Are they on a timer?"

"I have no idea. I've never been here this late."

Roxie glanced at her watch and saw it had just turned midnight, so that was probably what happened. Cheyenne worked at this office for years but didn't recall this. Maybe they had changed the switches for efficiency.

The reason they were both there so late was because the FBI wanted all evidence transferred to their laboratory division in Quantico, Virginia. It would happen in seven hours.

Le Blanc was a ten-year veteran of the department and caught a break when Cheyenne transferred to Kalispell. She had fought for Denton's old job, basically throwing herself into the role, and with Cheyenne's recommendation, she got it.

That was just a year ago, and here she was, working on the highest profile case of her career. There was no way she was going to screw this up, which was why Cheyenne was helping.

Roxy had logged in to the JusticeTrax Laboratory Information Management System, so on her screen, the windows for their program, and the national DNA programs were open.

She was double and triple checking to see that all the tags matched, and all physical evidence had an electronic match. Cheyenne observed her to make sure nothing was missed. The evidence itself was lined up on a stainless-steel table outside the office and they had already gone through it.

"I better turn the lights back on. If Abe walks by, I don't want him to think we already left." She was referring to Abe Kaufman, tonight's security guard, who had stopped by an hour or so before.

"I can do it," Cheyenne offered.

"No, let me. I have to stretch my legs."

Roxy rose wearily and was across the room near the door when a dark shape approached her. Her first reaction was surprise, then a scream before she lashed out at the shadow.

There was no talking, no pleading or interaction whatsoever. A single shot from a suppressed pistol went through her outstretched palm and into the center of her chest as she flew backward. Her life was extinguished before her head slammed into the floor.

Cheyenne was staring at the monitor when she heard the scream, followed by the distinctive sound of a muted gunshot. In a panic, she quickly put the monitors into sleep mode, throwing the entire morgue into darkness, with the only light coming from the green exit sign above the door. Low to the ground, she stealthfully exited the office, heading toward the morgue lockers.

The two dark shapes parted as one headed to the evidence table, the other toward the room where Cheyenne had just been.

Across the room now, Cheyenne paused at the morgue lockers and slowly reached inside the front of her jeans. She placed her hand around the grip of her small handgun and slowly pulled it out of the carbon fiber holster. Cheyenne could shoot many guns but had never shot a human being. Knowing Roxy was down, they were going to kill her, or she was going to kill them.

From her hiding place, she watched the dark shape enter the room where she had been when a second man approached him, their silhouettes barely visible.

"Do it," he said, "I'll find the other one."

The man at the computer snapped the monitors back on and entered each application, deleting every file of evidence related to the Bartholomew case. Afterwards, he then emptied all contents of the computer's recycle bin, knowing there were backups, but that was someone else's problem.

The second man headed to where Cheyenne had been. At the morgue lockers, he started to open each one, thinking she was hiding there.

Cheyenne silently walked back further until the room ended, and she found herself stuck in a corner where they kept the various scales, saws, and other autopsy equipment.

The man who had been in the office was now at the stainless-steel evidence table. Under the glow from the exit sign, he began to place each evidence bag methodically into a large daypack that had been on the floor.

All that work, she thought, as he hoisted the pack on his shoulder and shouted to the other shadow, "Time to go."

"I'll find her. Give me a minute."

"Not important, time to go," he barked.

And the two shapes headed toward the door, when the sound of the elevator just outside the outer doors filled the room.

A minute later, the lone security guard, Abe Kaufman, had finally made his way down to the basement level. Of all the areas he patrolled, the morgue level was the one area he hated the most; they all did. From the strange sounds, cold air, and smells he would never get used to, this entire area gave him the creeps, especially late at night.

In the back of the room, Cheyenne heard the elevator stop, thinking to herself, *Abe, please not now, just go away.*

If she could time it, maybe she could jump up and fire a shot to alert him, but her Glock wasn't suppressed. In this tile and stainless-steel room, it would be exceptionally loud.

Abe had exited the elevator, noting the hall lights were off. He inserted the special key that turned the lights back on. Walking around the corner, he wondered if the girls were still there.

Sure enough, the morgue lights were out, so the girls must have gone home.

Abe peered through the double doors and noticed the office light was off, but the computer monitors were still on. The protocol was strict here, and you could never leave your workstation without logging off. The girls must have been dog-tired and forgotten. From inside the morgue, the hallway lights were allowing the gunman to see out, but Abe could not see in.

Just the thought gave Abe the creeps, but he would have to log them off and entered the first door into the vestibule of the morgue. He was just about to click on the lights inside the room when he saw what looked like a body on the floor. The shape was bathed in the green light from the exit sign. It was Roxy Le Blanc.

Stunned, he jumped back, yelling, "Holly shit."

He unsnapped his service revolver and pulled it out of his holster when suddenly, the face of a man dressed in black appeared just outside the glass door.

From across the room, Cheyenne had heard Abe and could see the gunman in the green light. Without hesitation, she fired twice at the gunman, then dropped back down.

As she imagined, the acoustics of the stark room amplified the sound so loud she momentarily couldn't hear a thing. The bullets slammed into the man's back and right shoulder as he flew forward, his own gun sailing through the air before it landed and skidded across the slick floor.

The second man brought up a pistol and fired through the glass, hitting Abe multiple times before he could shoot, as he crumpled to the floor in a heap.

The same gunman turned and fired at Cheyenne. One bullet hit the top of the gurney, and a second came in lower, missing her thigh by an inch. She jumped up and fired three more shots at him just as the other shadow grabbed the backpack and ran out of the vestibule.

Once again, the gunman at the door should have gone down, but he just turned, shrugged his shoulders and in the green glow, he smiled.

The fuckers were wearing armor.

He raised his pistol and fired again at Cheyenne. She tried to drop but waited too long when the first bullet hit her in the arm, and she screamed in pain. The second slammed into the top of her head and she fell backward to the ground with a thud.

The two killers had not expected to encounter the technicians or the security guard, so it would have made sense to head straight for their safe house. But they weren't done yet.

Turning off the hall lights, they retraced their steps and exited the building, walking casually back to their car. There they entered and drove the eighty miles from Missoula to Kalispell to obtain the evidence there.

Chapter 17

North Miami, Florida

Janice Hayward sat in front of a computer monitor in her apartment when her phone buzzed. It was just after one in the morning when she yawned, waiting for the text she knew was coming.

Seconds later, one of the guys in Montana texted: "Done. Do your thing."

For the past six years, Janice had been doing freelance work to earn money and was about to make some more. It took minutes to hack into the primary server of the Forensic Science Division substation in Missoula.

Knowing nothing of the harm the two had caused, she only knew that when summoned, she was to remove the entire backup from the previous four days.

As soon as she finished, she entered a second server for the Forensic Science Division substation in Kalispell and did the same thing.

Her entry into their system would be uncovered, but she was too good to get caught. She smiled, knowing they would try, but her access had been routed around the world. It would take someone highly proficient to get through just half of the locations.

And even if they did, she had a little surprise for them as she turned off her computer to get some sleep, a few thousand dollars richer.

Back in Missoula, Cheyenne's rapid breathing was the only sound in the room other than the humming of the morgue lockers as she tried to right herself. She didn't think she had been unconscious for very long, but needed to check on Roxy and Abe. Feeling a sharp pain in her arm, she held on to the stationary gurney, feeling dizzy. She suspected she had likely lost a lot of blood and possibly had a concussion from the head wound.

She grabbed a small rubber strap, wrapped it around her arm to slow the bleeding, and held a towel softly against her scalp. The head wound had bled like crazy at first, but was slowing as she headed to Roxy on wobbly legs, fearing the worst.

She kneeled down but didn't have to check for a pulse. It was obvious she was gone. With a sob, Cheyenne gave her a kiss on the shoulder that mixed with her tears as she shook her head softly, trying to accept that her friend was dead. It just made her dizzier.

Righting herself, she walked to the door, thinking Abe was there, but he wasn't, and at first, she thought perhaps he had escaped harm, but the glass was everywhere. She looked inside the vestibule and saw him crumpled on the floor. She stepped over the broken door and felt his neck, and smiled.

He had a faint pulse. She held his head and gave him a light shake, asking, "Abe, can you hear me?" She tried several times, but he didn't respond so she reached over and grabbed his comm device off of his shoulder unsure of who it actually conversed with.

Pressing the talk button, she said, "Hello. This is an emergency. Someone help me, please."

"This is Anderson Security dispatch. Who is this?"

"My name is Cheyenne Denton. I'm a CSI from Kalispell. I'm here at the Forensic Science Division substation in Missoula. Two gunmen shot our security guard, Abe Kaufman, and killed the lab tech, Roxy Le Blanc. Abe is still alive, but he needs immediate medical attention. I see three separate gunshot wounds."

"And you are with him?"

"Yes."

"Are you injured?"

"Yes, two gunshots, but they are not life-threatening."

"Stay with him, and the police will be there in a few minutes. Where are you in the building?"

"We're in the morgue. It's on the basement level."

"Are the gunman still there?"

"I don't think so."

"Stay next to the comm device and keep me informed, Okay?"

"Yes. Tell them to hurry."

Chapter 18

Jenkins Residence, Kalispell

Jenkins awoke to the buzzing sound of his phone and wearily noted it was just after three in the morning. Agent Stone was calling, which couldn't be good.

"Jenkins," he said sleepily.

"It's Stone. Meet me at my office."

Jenkins didn't hesitate and rose from the bed, throwing on the same clothes from the previous day, and headed out to his truck. Stone's office was close to his own station, and he parked just outside the main doors. When he tried the doors, they were locked, but a disheveled Stone came around the corner and pushed one open, letting him in.

"What do we have?" Jenkins asked.

Stone looked at him and seemed genuinely concerned. "We've got just a few hours before all hell breaks loose. Approximately two hours ago, a lab tech was murdered down in Missoula, and your CSI and a security guard were injured. Him seriously."

"Cheyenne?" Jenkins asked.

"Yes. The victim is Roxy Le Blanc, and your CSI got hit in the arm and a graze on her head. The security guard was shot three times and is in critical condition. If I had this right, Le Blanc and Denton were there getting the Bartholomew evidence ready for transfer to Quantico, which would have taken place later this morning. According to Denton, who has given a statement, two gunmen entered, killed Le Blanc, and stole the physical evidence related to the Bartholomew case. They also erased all files. The security guard was about to enter the morgue when Denton engaged the gunman. She hit him twice, but he was wearing armor. One ran out with the evidence, and the other shot the security guard before he could get off a shot. Denton hit him three more times, but then he got her."

"So, we have no blood evidence of the killer?"

"If I understand it correctly, we have no physical evidence at all."

"But our office here in Kalispell has backups, right?"

"Unknown. While the evidence was being removed, someone also got into their system and removed the backups. My team says these are insiders."

Billy sighed, knowing this was a step backward and a personal hit. "We need to find out if Kingman's office has a backup file of the original sample. I also need to tell Richard. He and Cheyenne are close."

"What do you mean close?"

"I mean close. Whoever is behind this at Cartwright is a fucking dead man."

"Jenkins, this can't become personal."

"It's already happened, Stone. Saddle up or get the hell out of the way."

"Fuck it, I'll likely be off the case by morning, anyway."

A few hours later, Damion Caruso had just pulled into the FBI parking lot and exited his car, looking much like the bastard he really was. Tall, broad shouldered, he walked with purpose, his enormous arms sticking out slightly from his side because they were too large to hang straight down.

Not everyone big had a powerful gait, but Caruso had mastered his. When he walked, it was always powerful, focused, and added to the scowl on his face, only a complete idiot would dare approach him.

Caruso was the Special Agent in Charge of the Resident Agency for Flathead. The same building where Special Agent Stone had set up shop. Flathead County itself was a large territory with extensive rural areas, and Caruso traveled often. Provided, of course, it was a high-profile case.

Most recently, he had been up north on a case involving the murder of two college students. The case had high media coverage, so he had jumped at the chance. He had cleared that case when the murder of Bartholomew happened here, and he quickly summoned Special Agent Stone to Kalispell.

Bringing in Jeremy Stone had been a calculated risk, since he knew far more about this case than anyone would ever imagine. What could not happen was for this to get solved quickly, meaning he needed a fall guy.

On his drive down back to Kalispell, Caruso had just received word about the evidence loss with two wounded and one dead. The body count was now four, with two wounded. The case was escalating as he assumed it would, and he needed to get this back in order before he effectively lost control, which could not happen.

Not with this case.

As he entered the station, he received a few nods from the team, although most left him alone. Going directly to Stone, he said quickly, "What do we have?"

None too happy to see Caruso, Stone reiterated the last three days, and, on the surface, Caruso saw far more evidence than he had been led to believe. Not that it mattered. Four dead and growing.

He turned to face Sheriff Jenkins.

"Jenkins, what are you doing here?"

"Giving Stone an assist."

Caruso looked at Stone. "What the fuck, Stone, we have fifteen people here. Why would you delegate outside the team?"

Turning to Jenkins, he added, "Listen, Jenkins, no offense, but Christ, this is a high-profile case. We need to own this. I'm sure you understand."

"Still a political asshole, I see," Jenkins replied as Stone tried to conceal his smile. Jenkins and Caruso had a history, and Jenkins was not a fan.

"Excuse me, what the fuck did you just say?" Caruso barked.

"Save it, Caruso. While you were on the television, we have lived this case with over sixty hours of case time. We're starting to make progress."

"Oh, sure. Great progress increasing the body count, but somehow, you're nowhere close to solving this, Sheriff. Perhaps your *bromance* with Special Agent Stone is why the case has stalled. This is an FBI matter and clearly far above the minds of local law enforcement. Out!" he yelled. Without a word, Jenkins grabbed his hat, nodded to Stone, and left.

Caruso saw the nod between them. "Are you still with us, Stone, or do you want to continue playing deputy with Jenkins?" He said in the most condescending tone possible. "I can even arrange that full-time."

Two hours later, Stone was in Caruso's office, mildly prepared for the critique he knew was coming. It would take his best behavior not to get kicked off the case. It was no surprise that Caruso was a hothead, and, as Jenkins had already said, his aspirations were much higher than being the SAIC of Kalispell, Montana.

Caruso barked, "What were you thinking, Stone? Bringing Jenkins in on the case screams amateur hour. You alienated the team."

"Just as you did when you brought me in from down south."

Ignoring the jab, he barked, "He's not one of us, Stone. There is a huge difference."

"I got that. I rode him and his friend Richard Chase hard, but you know what? These guys are good, and I've been using them to broaden our efforts. We have pieced together a great deal of information, and we're close to a breakthrough."

"Breakthrough? How? You have no evidence of the killer, and you have no admissible evidence of Cartwright & Cartwright, and one death is now four. What you have is jack-shit in a case that is soon to get national attention."

"I respectfully disagree. What we are doing is making someone very nervous. They'll screw up soon, and we'll have them."

"Bullshit. Time to pack it up, Stone. You had your chance on a high-profile case and blew it."

Stone stood, visibly angry. "If you want me off, Caruso, then you take me off."

"Who the fuck do you think you're talking to?" Caruso yelled, red-faced, and stood, getting up inches from Stone's face. Everyone outside the office had turned to see them argue, but wisely turned away.

Stone was many things, but intimidated wasn't one of them as he stared Caruso down before replying.

"Who am I talking to? I thought I was talking to the same guy that brought me here. You know, so if this went to shit, he would have a guy to blame it on. But I accepted the assignment anyway because I know how to solve cases and do what I'm told. And now, two hours after you finally show up, you're ready to pull me. Go ahead, I fucking dare you to own this."

"If you ever talk to me in that tone again, Special Agent Stone, I'll have your ass. You won't be able to issue a fucking parking ticket."

"Save it for someone who doesn't know you, Caruso," Stone replied, holding his ground.

No doubt, Caruso would eventually move up and likely haunt Stone his entire career. But he also knew that down in the trenches, it was guys like him, Jenkins, and even Chase that always got the damn job done. Caruso would not fire him.

"Get the fuck out of my office and solve this case, or your ass is mine," Caruso yelled.

Chapter 19

Providence St. Patrick Hospital, Missoula

It had taken just fifteen minutes to transport Cheyenne and Abe Kaufman to the Providence St. Patrick Hospital in Missoula. Kaufman had been rushed to surgery, and it was unclear if he would make it with a leg wound, a stomach wound, and most serious, an upper chest wound.

Cheyenne had been taken into the emergency room and received eighteen stitches in her head. The bullet in her arm had passed through the top of her biceps, and while it hurt like hell, she would regain full use of it in time.

The Missoula FBI had already taken her statement, as well as the local police, and according to the head nurse, Jenkins and Stone would arrive soon. She had hoped to see Richard, but assumed with all that had happened, he wouldn't drive down.

After the altercation with Caruso, Stone had picked up Jenkins and was seriously exceeding the speed limit as they drove down to Missoula in Stone's Escalade SUV. With the blue lights flashing, they arrived at the hospital in a little over an hour, which was not bad for an eighty-mile trip.

They both entered her room, and Jenkins led since he knew her formally. "Morning Cheyenne. You are one brave and lucky lady."

"I've thought a bit about the lucky part more than once, Billy. Hello Agent Stone."

Stone nodded. "How are you feeling?"

"I'm okay," as tears formed in her eyes. "It's the loss of Roxy and the condition of Abe that I can't shake. I mean, all this for some fucking blood evidence?"

"The killer obviously is someone special enough to warrant such precautions," Jenkins replied.

"Meaning Bartholomew's killer wasn't a hired hand like these guys," Cheyenne said.

"Exactly," Stone replied.

It was another thirty minutes before Cheyenne had given them the same story given to local police and the Missoula FBI. They said their goodbyes to let her rest and allow the pain medication to take hold.

As they walked out of the emergency area toward the lobby and primary waiting room, Chase was just walking in.

"Hey guys, what do we know?"

"Hey Richard. Glad you were able to make it down," as Jenkins reiterated what had happened.

Chase said in wonder, "That is a lot of risk just to hide blood evidence."

"We just had the same conversation. The killer is someone they don't want us to know about," Jenkins added.

Almost as if he couldn't help himself, Stone said, "Hey Chase, I know this hits home, but stay with us, okay? It won't help if you go all vigilante here."

"I get it, Stone, but this is personal, and those responsible are going to pay," Chase said, although he didn't voice what he was really thinking. *This was now an eye for an eye. You shot one of mine. I'm gonna shoot two of yours.*

Richard left the guys went up to see Cheyenne. As he entered, the room contained two beds, but only one was occupied. Other than the nasal cannula, she looked perfectly normal. Her dark complexion was a stark contrast to the white bedding, and her right bicep was heavily bandaged, as was her head.

Just as he approached the bed, she opened her eyes and smiled.

"Hey. Sorry to wake you. I just wanted to say hello."

"I was just dozing. Between the medication and the questions, it wore me out. I didn't expect to see you here."

"Yeah, well, I was in the area. I'm so very sorry about your friend."

Cheyenne tilted her back into the pillow. "In the area, right?" Saddened, she began to tear up again.

"Poor Roxy. I should have saved her. Instead, her scream saved me. And Abe, shit, I thought if I could one of them, he could take out the other. But they were wearing armor. I don't think he even got off a shot."

"I know what it's like to lose a friend, but you did all you could. You're very lucky to be alive."

"Maybe. If I could have only got a headshot, I might have been able to save Abe, at least."

"Well, think that, if it makes you feel better. I'm just glad you're alive," Richard replied.

"Any word on Abe?"

"I saw Jenkins on the way in, and he said he was still in surgery. It's critical, but he's still alive."

"Any leads?"

"Regarding today, no. Every day, we get closer, and trust me when I tell you they will pay dearly for this."

"Do me a favor."

"Anything."

"Don't get yourself killed."

"Hadn't planned on it." He smiled, and her eyes slowly closed, and he soon left her to rest and drove back to Kalispell.

On the way back to Kalispell, Stone had called Dr. Kingman to update him on Cheyenne, but also to ask about the local evidence.

"Dr. Kingman, can I assume that the blood DNA evidence has backups at your office?"

"Yes. We do not have physical samples, but we have the original notes and the electrograph. I guess we need to secure it quickly. To be honest, it was the last thing on my mind."

"I know. We're a few miles out. We'll meet you there and make sure it has a safe home."

"It does, but fine, as you wish. I'll meet you there."

As soon as Stone entered the parking lot, both he and Jenkins knew they were too late. Both sheriff's SUVs from Jenkins station were there, engines running, lights flashing.

Stone didn't bother with a parking space and flipped on his flashing blue light as he and Jenkins headed to the entrance.

Deputy Mcloud was there.

Jenkins asked. "What happened, Ben?"

"Break-in, sir. Someone got into the evidence room. I tried to call you earlier."

"We were in Missoula, just got back," Jenkins said as they met Dr. Kingman and followed him in.

Deputy Thompson was standing outside the room when Jenkins and Stone came down the hall and looked past him at the door. The lock was smashed, and the steel safety plate on the door was almost ripped off.

"Did you touch anything, Scott?" Jenkins asked.

"No, but I left a message for Cheyenne to come in and see what was taken."

Jenkins looked down and said softly, "Scott, Cheyenne has been shot, but she'll be fine. Unfortunately, we know exactly what they took."

Kingman heard the comment and went off to get another CSI to process the room.

Chapter 20

FBI Resident Agency, Kalispell

Inside his office, a phone buzzed inside the jacket pocket of Damion Caruso. He had two phones, one for the agency and another, a burner phone he used for other dealings. Although he rarely carried it on his person, he knew to do so today after the news of the Missoula incident reached him. He glanced at the number even though he already knew who it was.

A woman's voice said curtly, "For an agent not expecting to make progress, Stone is getting very close."

Caruso shook his head. "It's like he's a different guy. Normally, he works alone and pisses off the locals so much it takes forever to solve anything," he said defensively.

"So, you picked the right guy, but underestimated Sheriff Jenkins and Richard Chase," she replied.

"Perhaps, but they're just fishing. They have no tangible evidence, and what they have is not admissible. Besides, I broke up their little party."

"I don't have to explain to you what will happen if they tie this together."

"I know that, but you're not helping. That mess down in Missoula was a colossal mistake. My command wants this solved yesterday, and I assure you, Jenkins and Chase are going to make this personal. At some point, even I won't be able to stall them."

"Well, you better. You're being paid to make sure this case is not solved. That is your only objective, so be creative and ruthless."

"I'm working on it. It will be okay."

"I lack your confidence. Work harder," she yelled, and the call ended.

Chapter 21

Fortitude Security, Kalispell, Day Four

Chase headed back to the Kalispell and arrived after ten that same morning. Part of him had wanted to stay with Cheyenne, but his gut said, get back to the team.

As he arrived at the house, Richard went straight to Fortitude. Minutes later, Alex entered. "Hey, boss, you wanted to see me."

"Yeah, I need a quick favor," as he explained what had happened to Roxy and Cheyenne.

"This is horrible. I'm so sorry. What do you need?"

"Try to find out how they got into the server, and if possible, try to follow it back to whoever they are. Let me know if you find anything."

Alex nodded and walked out to go downstairs, and Eddy entered a few minutes later.

"Have a seat, Eddy."

"What's up?"

"Any calls related to the burner phone in Griffin and Bartholomew's neighborhood?"

"No. I set up small triangulation devices signaling off the main cell tower. If the same phone is used, it will register a possible hit to within one hundred feet, but so far, nothing."

"What about the principals from the Trinity LLC?"

"No news."

"Any luck on tying Pullman to a flight into Glacier Airport?"

"His name was not on any commercial or private flights in the two days leading up to the murder. Only two private planes came in, and both checked out to owners who are still here."

Frustrated, Chase leaned back. "Shit. We're four days in, and the FBI is getting nervous." He then told Eddy about Roxy and Cheyenne and lost DNA evidence. "Stone is under pressure, meaning if we can't crack this, all hell is going to break loose soon. We need a break, and the biggest potential leads we have are that burner phone and the identity of the three principals from Trinity. See what you can do to step it up."

"On it," Eddy said as expected and paused at the door. "I'm sorry about Cheyenne, but she's tough, and we're going to get these assholes."

"Thanks, Eddy," Chase said, trying not to reflect on what had happened but rather, what needed to happen.

From her office, Alex started to hack into the Forensics Division server. Since it had been breached, the system was currently offline, with only a shell running internally. But she didn't need to access the functional system, just the code behind it.

She gave pause to the fact that the team there might be able to see her, but she assumed correctly that the forensic teams were not there yet. Even if they were and saw her, she'd just bug out. There was not an easy trail for them to follow her back to Kalispell.

As her fingers flew across the keyboard, she went to a series of patches that someone had made from outside the network. These were likely employees or contractors who had fixed bugs remotely, but this was also where a hacker might have been able to enter. That is what she would have done.

Searching the code of each patch, it was two hours later when she pumped her fist and grabbed a memory stick, placing it into her USB port. The purpose was to put a trace program on the incoming server. If the original hacker was good, they would be ready for this, having installed a program to bounce off if she found the location. But if the trace program was home grown, there was a chance the location would be visible for a few seconds.

Alex stared at the screen not moving a muscle. For hours, it searched the world, which was not an exaggeration. The trace was in the cyberworld, bouncing from server to server, all around the world as it sought to find the origin. Thankfully, the computing power of Fortitude was far from average.

The day was almost over when it stopped, just for a second, and Alex immediately picked up the phone and called Chase.

"What do you have?" he asked

"They got in from a private network in North Miami, Florida."

"Can you find who the network belongs to?"

"Not if they are any good, but I'll try."

"So, it's definitely not a company like Cartwright & Cartwright?" Chase said, hoping it could be that easy.

"No, this is a home network or possibly an internet kiosk. It is linked to a Verizon tower in North Miami, but the user created a virtual private network (VPN) to mask themselves."

"But you can get into that, right?"

"Um, maybe. They used a service called Mullvad. Unlike most VPN services, when you set up their account, they don't require any personal information. Instead, they issue the user a random account number that doubles as your login credentials. Even if I can get the number, at best, it will only be linked to a credit card number."

"Unless you get into the Mullvad system."

"Of course, but that could take days, not hours."

"Keep at it, but be careful," Chase said, dejected.

Eddy grabbed a piece of paper and ran upstairs about as fast as anyone had ever seen him move. He headed straight for Chase's office and ran in, surprising him as he did so.

"My triangulation system got a hit," he said quickly.

"Same phone?" Chase said in amazement.

"Yeah, the same phone just called another burner phone."

"Which house?"

Eddy set the paper he had been waving down in front of Chase. "The dot is the center of the triangulated signal."

Chase looked at the picture showing a satellite image of the two homes at the end of a cul-de-sac, about two hundred feet from each other at the closest point. Dead in the middle was the dot.

"Shit. It could be either house."

Eddy added, "It seems a little closer to the Bartholomew house."

"Thanks, Eddy, but both houses are under suspicion, so either could be the suspect. We can't guess."

"I'm sorry, I thought it would ping closer, but ..."

"Eddy, it's okay. You did well. We'll see where it leads."

Chapter 22

Takuetsu Sushi Restaurant, Miami

Sitting in the back of the small, hip Sushi restaurant near their office, Enrique Alvaro and Alycia Gomes sat nervously. They were sharing a bowl of spicy green beans and edamame, although neither was hungry. But they needed a place outside the office to talk.

Alycia had mentioned the FBI agent to Enrique, who then shared that the same agent had been sent to him. Both had done exactly what they had been trained to do. Although Enrique wasn't concerned, Alycia was on the verge of freaking out.

"Alycia, seriously, you've got to calm down."

"It's the fucking FBI, Enrique. If they could talk to us, it's because they are following us. The FBI is following us!"

"Alycia, this is the same agency who is on a perennial mission to find dirt on the firm but never can. We know someone hacked into Trinity, and that's how they got our names, meaning it was probably them that hacked in. We said what we were told to say, and you told Decco about the hack. This has nothing to do with us."

"Enrique, how can you just blow it off like it's no big deal?"

"Because it's not."

"Well, I feel like I'm in danger, like I'm being watched."

"Why? You have done nothing wrong, and all those deals are legit."

"One of the names the agent used was 'Phoenix' and, as you know, that was a pseudonym for a former senator, Winston Bartholomew. I saw an article yesterday that he was murdered a few days ago."

"Okay, so what? Lots of Trinity files contain the name 'Phoenix' and have nothing to do with him. It's just a certain type of investment."

"We don't know that, but it says to me they're investigating his murder, and if the firm finds out they approached us, we are as good as dead."

"I disagree, but if you're right, then we tell them together. No secrets, right?"

"I'm too nervous. They'll see that, and they'll think I'm involved."

"Alycia, that is bullshit. Relax, and tomorrow, we'll tell Decco together."

She calmed down. "Thanks, Enrique. I know I'm a worrier, but with you there, I can do this."

"That's my girl."

From a car parked near the restaurant, both were being watched although neither had a clue. It wasn't possible to know what they said, but it was clear something had happened and that the guy was trying to calm the girl down.

Alycia Gomes arrived home nervous, although not as bad as she had been. Her apartment was in a ten-story low rise that had the Miami modern art déco flare, although she would love something larger but didn't have the budget for it. Not that she wasn't well paid at Cartwright, she was. But with almost two hundred thousand dollars in student loans, it was like she was paying for two apartments every month.

She entered the apartment and closed the door behind her, locking it with the deadbolt and chain. Her keys plopped into a bowl near the door, and she snapped on the light. From there, she headed for the refrigerator and pulled out a light beer. As soon as she made it into the living room, she froze, and the can of beer dropped out of her hand.

Sitting in her lounge chair was FBI agent Veronica Williamson.

"What are you doing here? You can't be here," Alycia yelled.

"Alycia, pick up your beer and have a seat. Nobody saw me, nobody knows I'm here, and you are safe."

She was about to tell the agent she was dead wrong when she caught herself, knowing she should not reveal what she thought she knew or how she felt. Instead, she said, "What do you want?"

"Information about the Trinity transactions and specifically those codenamed 'Phoenix.' I can protect you, Alycia. I know you're scared, but I can protect you."

"You can't, but it doesn't matter. I know nothing about Trinity."

"They have coached you to say that, but how long can you wake up every morning being afraid for your life, Alycia? You're a young, beautiful girl. You recently passed the bar. Don't you wish for more?"

"Please. I can't help you. You have to go."

"Alycia, I can help you. I know you want help. Let me do this for you."

"Do what?"

Agent Williamson saw the opening. "Another agent is downstairs. Let us take you to our office, and you'll never be threatened again. I promise you."

"Are you out of your fucking mind? Me, walk into an FBI office?"

"Are they watching you, Alycia?"

"Of course, you idiot. You just being here is going to get me killed."

"Alycia, I can help you."

"No, you can't. You have already signed my death warrant. Get out!" As she pointed angrily at the door.

From the scope of the high-powered sniper rifle, an assassin assessed the situation through the open blinds in the apartment of his target, Alycia Gomes. He was on a rooftop at level height three hundred yards away.

From where he was, it was clear the FBI Agent had entered without being invited, and the young attorney was surprised. But wisely, it appeared she had told the agent off and was now escorting her out.

He carefully moved his trigger finger away from the trigger and set down the rifle, wondering if she had any idea how close to death she had just been.

Chapter 23
Chase Residence, Kalispell

It was half-past nine when Stone arrived at the only place he seemed to find a dialogue to his liking, which surprised even him. He parked in Chase's driveway and walked around the back to find them out by the fire.

Chase said without looking up from the flames, "Beers inside. Better stuff is on the bar. Help yourself."

Stone, wearing a heavier jacket this time, just nodded and walked inside before returning with a beer. He slid it into a cozy cup holder to keep his hands from freezing as he sat in one of the oversized teak chairs.

He opened his beer, "Today could not have gone much worse. Caruso handed me my ass this morning, and we failed to recruit one of the attorneys involved with Trinity in exchange for protection. Do either of you guys have anything new?"

Jenkins shook his head as a no. "My entire day was a waste. Brass had me backtracking the evidence we had already obtained, and it took most of the day. We're zero for two, Richard, anything?"

"Mixed day. We still have nothing regarding the real identity of the principals to Trinity Holdings and have not been able to link Pullman to any flights in or out of Kalispell. On a positive note, we were able to trace the hacker that penetrated the Missoula Forensics server to North Miami, but they used a personal private network. We're trying to find the person's identity through the service, but it might not yield any personal information. We also were able to track another call from the burner phone in Griffin's neighborhood. Sadly, the triangulation wasn't accurate enough to point to which house, Griffin's or Bartholomew's."

"What do you mean, track another call?" Stone asked.

"If you recall, neither the phone records from Mark Griffin nor Katherine revealed any calls to numbers associated with Cartwright & Cartwright or Trinity Holdings. Well, yesterday, we broke into Cartwright's customer relations management system. These systems digitize phone calls and place them into text files so customer care can easily see the history of the caller. While Bernard Decco is not connected to the text conversion system, his phone is on their network, and that phone received a call from Bigfork two days ago. The signal came from the vicinity of the Griffin's neighborhood. One of my guys set up two fake towers near the real one to triangulate the call within a hundred feet if the same phone activated again. This morning, it did. A call went out from the same burner phone that called Decco, to somewhere in downtown Kalispell. Sadly, we couldn't determine which house the call came from, Griffin's or Bartholomew's."

"But the call went downtown. Where in downtown?"

"Same problem, a single cell tower will not give us a location. The closest we can pinpoint is somewhere within a mile radius of the cell tower downtown."

"Where is the tower located?"

"It's at Kalispell Regional Medical Center, northeast corner of the main parking lot."

Stone said with hope, "Have your team draw a map and determine what is within that radius."

Chase nodded.

"Why can't we just get a warrant to search both houses and find the damn phone?" Jenkins asked.

"Both have lawyered up, and we'll never get a warrant because we can't tell a judge how we got the information regarding the call," Stone replied.

Chase replied, "We'll get something. Then we lean on them and make them do something stupid."

"Guys, I appreciate the support, but if we want to break this, we need to get real tangible evidence," Stone countered.

They all just nodded, understanding where they were.

"Do you think Caruso will pull you?" Jenkins said to Stone.

"He only brought me up to be a fall guy if the case went wrong, but I assumed I could crack this fast and get a win. Caruso is too political to lead the case himself, but he'll likely kick me off and then take one for the team and request the big guns. We'll all be shut out when that happens."

"So, tomorrow has to be a big day," Chase said optimistically.

Chapter 24

North Miami, Florida, Day Five

From a hole in the wall, computer kiosk on the corner of northeast 123rd and Seventh street, Janice Hayward had just arrived. She found her spot and sat down in front of a computer she had just rented for an hour. Although she preferred the solitude of her apartment, she came here when she needed absolute anonymity, and she wasn't the only one. The place was packed.

Today, she wasn't working on a new job. Instead, she was checking up on a job she had completed two days before–when she hacked into servers at two different Forensic Science Divisions. The job had been easy. Hack in and remove the backup files from two locations for the last four days, and get the login credentials of a CSI in Kalispell, Montana. She succeeded and earned two thousand dollars for less than thirty minutes of effort. But in her business, reputation was everything, and getting caught was the kiss of death. Since the place of business was a state agency, she thought it best to double-check that she was in the clear.

As she clicked her way back into their server, she headed straight to where she had hacked in and placed a memory stick into the aged desktop computer. She silently found the program she had left there and transferred it to the memory stick and quickly got out. She then opened the small file.

Hayward wasn't worried in the least and normally,' she wouldn't have risked going back in, but she had been well paid for this. It wasn't the first time she had worked for this client and hoped it wasn't the last.

Looking at the monitor, she suddenly frowned. Her agent program had been triggered, meaning someone had penetrated her entrance point. Janice had figured the FBI or some IT geek would try, which is why she placed the agent file to attack such an inquiry in the first place. But as she looked at the physical code of her program, there was a line of random characters, and at first, she was confused, having never seen this before.

She leaned over to the guy next to her, a friend. "Hey, can you take a look at this?" He nodded, finished what he was doing, and glanced over at the mishmash of symbols on her screen.

"Have you seen this before?" she inquired, pointing to the odd characters.

"Yeah. Someone placed a trace on your IP address, trying to find you. The file they embedded there has since been pulled back off. When they did, it left gibberish. Kind of like a hole in your code."

"But I used Mullvad."

"Smart. They would have got you if not,"

"So, I'm like good, right?"

"Yeah, I mean, what are they going to do, hack into Mullvad?" They both laughed.

A thousand miles away, Janice would have been surprised to know that Fortitude Security was trying to do just that. Mullvad AB was a wholly owned subsidiary of Amagicom AB out of Gothenburg, Sweden. Both small businesses had powerful and well-protected systems. Alex had started the effort, but eventually found herself over her head and went to see Eddy.

He looked up as she walked in. "What's up?"

She rolled her eyes and asked, "I'm trying to get into this company, but it's not like anything I have encountered. Can you help?"

"Can't. The boss has me on a special project."

"Me too. No worries, I'll tell him you refused to help me," knowing he just didn't want to be bothered and started to walk out.

Three years earlier, nobody except Chase had an office within Fortitude, and while Eddy was good, seriously good, he needed silence. Most hackers could just tune out the background noise, but Eddy just got frustrated. And a frustrated Eddy was harmful to those around him. So, with the team's blessing, Chase built him a small office.

Alex was at the door when Eddy surrendered. "Fine, bring it."

Alex returned to his keyboard and opened a new window where she brought up the location she had been at. He pondered about it for some time.

"Well?" she asked.

"You are correct. Different."

"Can you get me in?"

"Not sure. To get around this firewall, it's looking for a catchphrase."

"You mean like they expected hackers and are now fucking with us?"

"Pretty much, yeah."

"Any idea how to figure out what the phrase is?"

"Normally, you would apply a generator application, but I assume they know that and likely have a time-out mechanism that shuts you down after a few minutes. Who is this again?"

"It's a company out of Sweden. They supply virtual private networks, and their subscriptions do not use personal info, just a random number. I need to see the transaction to get something useful, like a credit card or email address."

"Mullvad, I know them."

"Then why did you ask?"

"Just a test."

"You're an ass."

"How original. Do you want my help or not?"

"Pretty please," Alex replied, with more than a little sarcasm.

Eddy went to work, and eventually Alex left him to it. It was two hours later when he came in with all smiles and placed a sticky note on her monitor. On it, he had written the user code and credit card number.

"How did you get in?"

"Easy," he said. "I just had to be better than you."

Alex ignored his attempt at humor, although he might have just said it because it was true. She immediately opened a file that took her to the dark web and went to a location she had used before. When companies have a data breach, the information taken can be for a specific reason or it might just be used to sell to others.

In this folder was a database of American Express card numbers, and she picked it because the number Eddy gave her only had fifteen digits. That meant an AMEX card. But after fifteen minutes of effort, her search did not find a match.

Going to another folder, she tried but failed again. On the next attempt, she went to a folder that contained older information and tried again. Bingo.

The credit card belonged to a woman named Janice Hayward who lived in North Miami Beach. It took Alex another half hour to locate her address, and she went up to see the boss.

"Hey, I found the person who hacked into the Forensic Lab. She's a hacker out of Miami and works for hire. I'm thinking I should go see her and try to get a contact name or number?"

"No way, Alex. These guys are playing for keeps, and Miami appears to be bad guy central. It's too much risk."

"Okay, how about this? Since she works for hire, what if we contact her on the dark web and offer her money for the contact info?"

"If this person had no personal integrity, it could work. But my guess is that she has a standing job with someone associated with Cartwright & Cartwright. Too risky."

"But there is no way she can trace me."

"Alex, you found her. I'm not saying you're not better, but can you really hide? This firm could have an entire team working on just this kind of stuff."

"Maybe, but between Eddy and me, I can assure you, she won't be able to find me."

"My gut is saying no, so that's the answer. Got it."

"Yep, got it."

As Alex walked away, Chase was concerned. Part of him wanted to stop her and tell her to go for it, but nothing he had said wasn't true. These guys had proven more than serious, so he let her go back to her office.

Jenkins had been sitting at the station when he had a thought. It was risky, but knowing time wasn't on their side, he grabbed a small device Chase had given him a year earlier. He powered it up and keyed a number into its small keypad before placing it inside one of the small leather pouches on the front of his gun belt. Soon after, he headed to his truck and drove to Bartholomew's house.

Once there, he parked after his deputy let him past the gate. The crowd of reporters was still there, although the overall number had diminished. Since Katherine refused to leave the house, it left them with no reward for their encampment.

At the door, he knocked and Katherine's neighbor, Angie Griffin answered, causing him to roll his eyes, and it was unlikely she missed his expression.

"Hello, Sheriff Jenkins," Angie said, all peaches and cream.

"Ma'am. Is Katherine home?"

"She is, but she is not receiving any callers today."

"I would like to hear that from her."

"Well, she deputized me to help her avoid the unfriendliness that law enforcement has taken toward her."

"She deputized you. Seriously. I'm just the local sheriff and a friend of the family, and I came by to see how she was doing. It won't take more than a few minutes of her time."

"So, when can we have that lunch to discuss crime and related topics for my book? As I believe I mentioned, you are the spitting image of my main character, Agent Zack Zamora."

"For the love of Pete ..." Jenkins said, stopping himself before he said how he really felt about the comparison. "Fine, Ms. Griffin. You win. I'll give you an hour once this case is solved. Only if you will let me say hello to Katherine."

"Call me Angie," she said with a huge smile. "See, that wasn't so hard. Please come in, and I'll get her."

Jenkins entered and walked as far into the house as he could. Katherine came down the stairs, and to his word, he only asked how she was holding up and if she needed anything.

"I'm okay. Thank you for keeping the reporters and that foul FBI Agent away from the house. Any luck making this all go away?"

"Honestly, Katherine. No. We believe Bart's death is tied to his investments, but we have little evidence from your husband or your brother to point the way. We just know their deaths seem related." Neither woman responded.

Katherine replied, "Since I've heard nothing new, I assumed that to be the case, but it's unfortunate because these parasites won't go away until you do."

He assumed she was referring to the reporters. Jenkins shuffled, feeling for her situation. "Well, if you can think of anything that might help, please call me."

"I will, and please ask Mr. Chase to call me. I was hoping he might give me a status report or something."

"I will. Ladies."

As he headed toward the door, he turned and asked, "Ms. Griffin is your husband at home, I had a question for him."

"As I understand it, you'll have to arrange that with his attorney."

"I know all about that. The question was not specific to this case. It was more of an investment question. A what if kind of thing?"

"Well, he is home, so you can try. Or you can ask me, and I can ask him."

"I'd prefer to ask him if he'll allow it, but thanks just the same."

As Jenkins headed to his truck, he jumped in and quickly checked the device. Nothing.

He then drove next door to the driveway of the Griffin home and went to the side door of the office complex, where he had exited days before. He knocked but got no answer, so he rang the bell.

The door opened, and, not surprisingly, the same older woman, Claudine something, stood with a scowl on her resting bitch face. Today, her business suit was in peach tones instead of the dark blue she had worn the first time he was here, but otherwise, she looked and acted the same.

"Good morning, Claudine. I apologize for the informality, but I wasn't aware of your surname."

"Because it was never offered to you, Sheriff Jenkins."

"Yes, ma'am. I'm here to see Mark Griffin."

"He is in a meeting and cannot be disturbed."

"Can I come in and wait for him?"

"No, you may not. I was told that any meeting with law enforcement must be set up through his attorney," she barked.

"I am aware of all that, but I have a question for him about investments, and it is not directly related to the case involving Winston Bartholomew."

She took a step back, and Jenkins took a chance and simply walked in. When she stopped and turned in shock, he continued past her.

"What are you doing?"

"What?" he said in surprise.

"You cannot be here. I made that perfectly clear."

"What the hell? When you stepped back, I took that as you were inviting me to follow. I mean, seriously, I said I would just wait."

"I did not invite you in, and you are not welcome to wait. You must leave."

"Fine, fine. I'll let myself out, but you, ma'am, could use a damn personality."

As he turned and left, Claudine smiled, happy she had managed the situation. Although she could not see his face, Jenkins was smiling as well.

He had gotten inside, even if only for a few minutes.

From the conference room, Mark Griffin had watched the exchange. While he was pleased Claudine had once again proven effective; he wondered why the sheriff was even there.

Chapter 25
Kalispell Sheriff's Station

Jenkins didn't pause and went straight to his truck without checking the device. He did so on the chance he was being recorded by the many cameras he had observed outside the house. Once he was clear of the cul-de-sac, he pulled over and removed the device from its pouch. He smiled as he looked down, noting the small red light was now green. The green light meant the locator had just confirmed that the prepaid phone was somewhere in the home office of Mark Griffin.

The same phone that called the law office of Cartwright & Cartwright and sent a call to downtown Kalispell.

After calling Chase and Stone, Jenkins returned to the Kalispell Sheriff's station, where they would soon join him. Chase got there first and walked in. "Nice job, Billy."

"Yeah, well. Might be something, might be nothing."

"I think it is something. Look at this."

Chase pulled out a picture of the microwave cell tower in the parking lot of the Kalispell Regional Medical Center. Around it was a red circle depicting a one-mile radius. Not surprisingly, it contained a wide area filled with businesses and homes. Smack dab in the middle was the resident agency office of the FBI.

He handed the picture to Jenkins. "This is the radius around the cell tower where the call was sent."

Jenkins looked. "The FBI office? It's just one of hundreds of probable locations within the radius. Hell, my station is in there, too."

"True. But their office would explain the fact that Cartwright seems to act on our information. Griffin talks to his FBI informant, who calls Florida. Then bam! Someone is dead."

"Come on, Richard, Stone, playing for both sides? Sure, I didn't much care for him at first, but shit, I'm just coming around."

"I never said it was him, but if it is?"

"Well shit, how do we play this? He'll be here in like five minutes."

"If he is part of this, we're dead if we tell him. If he's not, he is our only way inside, but I happen to agree with you. I don't think it's him."

"But what if he is?" Jenkins said just as Stone walked in.

"What if who is?"

"What?" Jenkins asked.

Stone replied. "You just said, 'But what if he is?' Who, Griffin?"

Jenkins looked at Chase, and Chase looked at Jenkins. Stone watched the exchange. "Okay, I've had enough bullshit for one day. What are you guys up to?"

Chase honestly did not see Stone as the informant and decided it was worth the risk to find out, and handed Stone the picture. Stone understood immediately.

"And how do you possibly figure that versus the hundred-plus other locations, it has to be my fucking office?" Stone barked, clearly pissed at the insinuation.

"It fits. We have wondered how Cartwright knows what we're thinking."

Stone snapped. "So, while I'm battling Caruso and risking my pension just to work with you two, you're here, making a case that the FBI is the informant for Cartwright. Do I have that right!" Stone screamed as his face turned crimson.

"Come on, Stone. It's no different than you would have done. We made no judgment. We're just following evidence," Jenkins hollered back.

Stone calmed down a little and sat. "Fair, but it's hard to accept someone in my own office is a traitor."

"You mean Damion Caruso's office," Chase added.

"Well, yeah, there's that," Stone said, giving thought to the possibility.

Back at Fortitude, Chase immediately got Eddy and Alex together and explained what Jenkins had found.

"So, what I'm looking for is anything that ties Damion Caruso to Mark Griffin or Cartwright. Can I assume Caruso has not shown up in your searches thus far?"

"Not for me," Eddy said.

Alex wasn't sure. "I don't recall it, but I'll check."

"Boss, what makes you so sure it's Caruso? I imagine he makes a decent wage and is a rising star, according to Stone. Wouldn't it make more sense that the insider is a disgruntled, underpaid analyst?"

"Eddy, the FBI, like most security businesses, compartmentalizes information. An analyst would have a piece of this puzzle but wouldn't know what the entire puzzle is. To me, the person informing Cartwright is someone in a capacity who knows this entire case. There are only two people there with that kind of knowledge. Stone and Caruso."

"So, should we also look into Stone?"

Chase nodded. "Probably. Do this. Eddy, you take Caruso, Alex, you take Stone. I need this today before Caruso overreacts and brings in a whole new team."

"On it!"

Chase watched them leave and felt guilty about having them research Stone. But hell, he'd only known him for less than a week, and as unpleasant as it might seem, there was always a remote possibility.

Glancing at the time, he noted it was just before noon, meaning it was three in the morning in Cavite City, the Philippines, where his wife of sorts, Darna, lived. It was too early to call, especially for the type of conversation he felt they needed to have.

Grabbing his Pendleton jacket, he left Fortitude and drove his truck up an old fire road on the south side of town. There, he parked, set up, and called his client, Katherine Bartholomew. Richard wasn't highly trustful of anyone until they earned it, and thus far, he had been on the fence with Katherine. His gut told him she knew more than she was saying.

The call went through and was answered. "Hello, the Bartholomew residence. How can I assist you?"

"This is Richard Chase. I need to speak to Katherine."

"Is she expecting your call, Mr. Chase?"

"Is that you, Ms. Griffin?"

"Call me Angie, and yes. Did you recognize my voice?"

"No, I just had an idea it might be you."

"But I was convincing, right?"

"Very much so. You should have been an actress." He said, appealing to her vanity, hoping it would shut her up.

"I performed in college, you know."

"Well, it certainly paid off. Can I speak to Katherine, please?"

"I'll bring her the phone; she was expecting your call. Hold on." Chase could hear her walking through the house, and the sound changed as her shoes left the marble, then the wood, and finally the carpet.

"Hello?"

"Katherine, this is Richard Chase. Billy said to call."

"Yes, I was looking for an update."

"Are you alone?"

"Why?"

"There are many moving parts to this investigation, and we cannot rule out anyone. I can talk to you, but not if Ms. Griffin is present." Katherine looked at Angie, who was sitting a few feet from her and lied. "No, she just left. Please continue, it's just me."

Chase smiled and told her of the loss of evidence and the death of the lab tech.

She replied, as one might expect. "My God, that is horrible. Those poor people. Does this loss of evidence mean the case is back to square one?"

"No. It makes it more difficult, but we're still making headway."

"I spoke with my brother Larry yesterday. He said the FBI had questioned him."

"They did, and he had little to offer. Like you, he was shocked to learn of Matthew's role in Trinity Holdings and that there was a relationship between them and Bart's investments. Even more surprising to him was that Trinity was tied to Cartwright & Cartwright. The very law firm the Senate, led by Bart, investigated years ago."

"If I didn't know better, I'd think Bart might have been fishing for information."

"You are not the first to say so, but why would you think that?"

"Mr. Chase, my husband, believed strongly in competition but more so in fair dealings. They were guilty, and he knew it, and he believed it was for political reasons they were exonerated."

"How so?"

"We'll never know, but the Florida senator during the investigation was part of a political dynasty. Some in his family wanted to back him in a national campaign after he won his second term. That was a first for a Florida Republican. Bart always thought that maybe Cartwright helped the family and then asked for a favor in return."

"Interesting, but not necessarily helpful, since the commission could not actually find a smoking gun, so to speak. And besides, Bart invested millions. That's an expensive way to get information."

"Bart never really cared about money. What really got to him was that the fine imposed on Cartwright was ridiculously low. Allowing them to have no admission of guilt made the Senate effort seem like a complete waste of taxpayer money. I doubt the firm even skipped a beat, but the Senators on that committee took a hit."

"I read up on that. Cartwright did an award-winning PR campaign."

"Yes, well, that was why Bart was more than curious. Do you think the FBI has more information than they are telling? It isn't a secret they don't warm up to locals like you or Sheriff Jenkins."

"That's always a possibility, Katherine."

"So, perhaps this is a colossal waste of money?"

"If you are referring to hiring Fortitude, it is your money, so I cannot advise you, but without us, you'll only receive what the Feds wish you to hear. They are running this investigation, but we are providing significant intelligence."

"I'm told if the case doesn't break open, they are bringing in a specialized team."

"We've heard the same, and you were so right when you said this was about more than Bart."

Katherine nodded, and they were about to hang up when he asked. "Katherine, how well do you know Mark Griffin?" She froze as she looked at Angie.

"Why do you ask?"

"Just curious."

"Not very well. I know his wife, of course, but Mark has never warmed up to me."

"Is that because of something you did or Bart did?"

"I don't understand."

"There has to be a reason he doesn't warm up to you. I just wondered if it was you or Bart," Chase said rather directly.

"Well, I can only assume it is me, since he seemed to like Bart. Is he a suspect as well?"

"Perhaps. He knows more than he is saying, but I could say the same about you."

"Mr. Chase, really. Do you treat all your clients with such disrespect?"

He smiled, knowing she would get pissed. "Only those that lie to me, Katherine. Say hello to Angie Griffin for me. If you hadn't noticed, she's standing right next to you on your right."

From his truck, Chase hung up. Glancing back through his scope through a large window into Bartholomew's second-story library, he chuckled at the shocked expressions on their faces.

Chapter 26
Fortitude Security, Kalispell

Richard had returned from his call with Katherine and met with Alex and Eddy, neither of whom appeared to have anything of substance. As he poured a fresh cup of coffee, he turned and asked, "So, nothing?"

Both looked at him, and Alex spoke first. "There was nothing from the advanced search I created relative to Stone and Griffin or Stone and Cartwright. There was a lot of press regarding past cases, and he's been doing this for a long time, over a hundred cases. On the dark web, I found a few criminal organizations who have included his name in correspondence and have more to go through. But thus far, it seems to me the context is that they want to hurt him more than about a relationship they might have with him."

"That makes sense. Keep on it." Richard glanced over at Eddy. "Eddy, what do you have?"

"I might have something, but I need more time."

"Like what?"

"I'd rather not say until I know," Eddy replied.

"We're running out of time, Eddy. What do you think you have? I won't act on anything you say until you have confirmed the intel."

He shrugged and said somewhat reluctantly, "Like Stone, Caruso has been at this for a while. Not nearly as many cases, but I found two where his name and Cartwright & Cartwright appear."

"So, there are cases where he is after them, or they are involved with his case."

"I'm not there yet. I need more time."

"Excellent. Get back at it."

An hour after they left, Richard looked at his watch. It was six in the morning in the Philippines and Darna would be up having coffee, so he reluctantly called, and she answered quickly.

"Hey! How are you?" she said in her usual sunny voice.

"Good. Busy with the case."

"How is it going? It's just been a week, right?"

"Five days and counting. It's turning out to be a complicated set of circumstances, made harder with the FBI running the show."

"They are more than capable," she replied.

"Maybe. This case has a lot of political tangents, but honestly, that is not why I called."

"Is Nathen okay?" Darna replied with worry.

"Yeah, sure. He's great. It was more about us."

"What about us, Richard? I love you; we just don't live together."

"I know that, Darna. It's just weird."

"Why is it suddenly weird? Have you found someone?"

"No, I mean, not really. It's just all work, no play gets old, and it's not like this is a new conversation."

"I know that, Richard. But to your comment, go ahead and play. I'm not possessive of you."

"I never said you were. It's just that sometimes it's nice to be with a woman instead of the guys, but I can't because it immediately makes me feel guilty."

"Why would you feel guilty? Richard, enjoy yourself. I don't mind."

"I can't believe you just said that. Like you won't mind."

"I don't think I would. Richard, I have made a choice, and I understand that has consequences. I think we will always love each other and be in each other's lives. But I never thought you should be celibate, waiting for me to change my mind. Have fun, enjoy. Just don't forget about me."

"We're man and wife, Darna. We have a son! How would I forget about you?"

"Oh my God, Richard, you're so old-fashioned. Yes, we are man and wife. Yes, we have a son, and I love you both. But I love many things."

"What, like other guys?"

"Would that bother you?" she replied, although Richard said nothing before she added, "Yes, of course it would. We are so different."

"Just so I'm clear, the reason none of this bothers you is that, in your eyes, we have an open marriage. How do we explain that to Nate?"

To Darna, her son would always be Nathen, and she refused to call him Nate.

"Nathen is very smart and very perceptive. He knows we are his parents, and that is all that concerns him. We will always be his parents, and nothing can change that."

"Wow, okay. I have to think about this. It's a bit out there for me."

"You're not mad at me, are you?"

He didn't answer the question. Instead, as his phone buzzed, he pulled it away to see who was calling. He came back on. "Listen, I have a call from the FBI. I'll call later, okay."

He looked back to the phone and answered the second call, disconnecting the call to Darna.

"What's up, Stone?"

"How did the call with Katherine go?" he asked.

Chase told him about the observed phone call to Katherine but did not mention the possible tie of Damion Caruso to Cartwright. He needed to be sure before he said anything.

Stone asked, "Nice work. What does Jenkins think of the girls as partners?"

"We haven't talked yet. It could be they are in this together, meaning it could be them rather than Mark Griffin making the calls. More likely, Angie

Griffin recruited Katherine to help her understand how we work for her book and let her in on the call."

"Or that all three are involved. Katherine wants to get back at her dismissive husband, and Griffin and his wife are in it for the money."

"What money? We haven't found any link between Winston's investments and Griffin."

"But if either Griffin or his wife are tied to Cartwright, then they are tied to the money."

"Maybe, but as far as we know, the Trinity documents did not say who, if anyone, was the beneficiary. Hell, it isn't even in Bartholomew's name. Maybe on death, it all goes back to Trinity and thus Cartwright."

Both gave that some thought.

Chapter 27
Cartwright & Cartwright, Miami

The elevator seemed to take forever as it rose from the sixth floor to the C-Suite on the twenty-eighth floor. Enrique and Alycia rode in the elevator, nervously silent, as it climbed before slowing and coming to a stop with a slight jerk. The doors opened, and their anxiety increased as they exited and made their way around the large bullpen as they headed for the outer offices.

This entire floor was for the owners and their executive team, so to staff-level employees like them, just being on this floor was a mixture of wonder and fear.

But going to the Bernard Decco's office brought that up a notch, as Enrique stopped in front of his receptionist and asked, "Good morning. We have an appointment with Mr. Decco at ten."

"Yes, Mr. Alvaro, he is ready for you. Please enter."

Enrique smiled, pleased she knew his name, and they entered his office. He was on the phone with his back to them, looking out over an amazing view of the ocean and the vast accumulation of wealth that lined the water's edge. They came toward his desk, and he turned slightly, motioning for them to sit, which they did as he ended his call.

"Good morning, Alycia, you look troubled. And Mr. Alvaro, I don't think we have met." Decco stood and reached out his hand. Enrique shook the massive outstretched hand that completely encircled his own. He wished his own wasn't so clammy and tried to offset that with a firmer grip and a vigorous shake.

Decco released his hand and sat, immediately squirting some sanitizer on his hand.

"So, why the nervousness," as he rubbed his hands together to work the sanitizer in thoroughly.

Alycia started to speak when Enrique jumped in. "We've been approached by the FBI."

"Really? Please tell me all about it," he asked casually.

"An Agent Williamson, Veronica Williamson, spoke to me at Starbucks and did the same to Alycia at a restaurant," as he handed Decco her card.

"She seems to know we were the signatories on some Trinity deals and wanted more explanation."

Decco looked at Alycia. "Do you think this is related to the Trinity hack a few days ago?"

"I think so, yes. This woman had obviously seen the files."

"Okay, but why would that make you nervous? I get it's not every day that a federal agent approaches you, but neither of you has done anything wrong."

"We know that and only said what we were told, but there's more."

Decco went from amused to curious. "Please explain."

It was then that Alycia told him about the agent in her home, trying to offer her protection in exchange for information. Of course, Decco knew all this since he had ordered the sniper on the roof as a precaution.

"Alycia, that must have been scary for you. Did this agent say what exactly she was trying to save you from?"

Alycia shook her head no.

"Are you sure? Her presence had to be for a specific reason." His gaze all but said she needed to tell him.

"She wanted to know about Trinity and the codename Phoenix and said she could protect me. I was too busy trying to get her out of my house to ask, but I can only assume she was referring to, you know ... our reputation."

Decco let out a chuckle. "Listen, I am aware of the persona that Cartwright has about being an enforcer, and there was a time when we actually worked hard to shut down such rumors. But after a while, we found it was good for business. It gave us a niche and a mystique that nobody could match. Seriously, people are afraid of us. Can you believe it?"

He loved watching them nod as if they couldn't believe it, knowing full well that they had both just peed their pants a little.

Standing now, he looked down at them. "Alycia, Enrique, thanks for letting me know. I'll look into this and make sure the FBI doesn't bother you again. Meanwhile, plug away, and please know that these rumors are just rumors. As you well know, it is not illegal to set up the tax havens we create nor to manage the money as we do for our high-net-worth clients. They are generally very important people who demand secrecy and discretion, and that is what we do. If anything else happens, let me know."

He did not shake their hands a second time, and they left. Arriving back in the elevator, the moment the door closed, Enrique said, "See, scaredy cat. I told you it was all good."

"I heard him, but something is not right about all this."

"He basically said don't worry about it, and here you are worrying."

"Listen, I won't go to Agent Williamson or anything, but seriously, something isn't right about those Trinity files, and the FBI knows it. I'm going to take another look at those transactions."

"Alycia, don't even think of accessing those files. Please, promise me you'll just drop this."

"Why? If we are so on the up and up, why not try? Your words would imply there is nothing to find. If that is the case, I'll back off," she said louder than she intended.

"Alycia, I know you're like a dog with a bone, but you have to drop this," he said, genuinely concerned for his colleague.

They said nothing more, and the door opened on the sixth floor, where they exited the elevator car.

As the door closed, Bernard Decco clicked off the speaker in his office, which was connected to a microphone in their elevator.

He liked this mousy young girl, but business was business. If she tried to access the Trinity files in their archive, she was dead.

Chapter 28

FBI Resident Agency, Kalispell

Special Agent Stone had walked in and headed to the evidence board where he had updated the information and then just stared at it, pondering its many implications.

He was so engrossed in thought that he had not heard Caruso's approach.

"It was a good day for you, Stone. Nobody died," Caruso said smugly.

Not skipping a beat, Stone replied, "A shame actually, I had my heart set on a certain someone."

"Petty Stone, really petty. So, it all seems centered around the Griffins and Katherine Bartholomew," Caruso said as a question.

"On the surface, there is means and opportunity, but not a compelling motive. Mark Griffin may or may not be involved in Bartholomew's investments but is now thought to be linked to the prepaid phone. If that is true, then he has a relationship with Cartwright. But even if he does, there does not appear to be any incentive or reason for him to kill Bartholomew, the same guy that handed him Conrad Point."

"Could his wife be the caller instead of him?"

"She can clearly act out the image she wants people to see. But her demeanor isn't compatible with what we know of Cartwright & Cartwright. I think she's a woman who always has to be the center of attention and has nothing to do with Winston Bartholomew."

"So, that leaves the victim's wife. Not the first time we have seen that."

"No, and we have thought of her since day one. She is related to both high-profile deaths who were also related to Trinity and, therefore, Cartwright. We also know she is clearly smarter than she has led everyone to believe. But to our knowledge, the only thing Bartholomew has done worthy of murder in her eyes was take her money, but I don't see how. The Pullman trust is ironclad, and he could not have accessed it without her, so either her brother helped him find a way, or she was involved and lied. Despite all effort, we can't find out which is true."

"And conveniently, the two that could help are dead."

"For that exact reason, I suspect," Stone said in agreement.

Caruso scanned the board and made a note of concern regarding the latest on the prepaid phone, some of which Stone had just added. "What is this about the burner phone? I thought the issue was it was used to call the law firm?"

"It did. But yesterday, the same phone called downtown Kalispell. The location was near the cell tower at the hospital."

"Where?" Caruso asked with caution.

"No idea, we can't pinpoint it further. It could be anywhere," Stone said, being purposely selective with his words.

"But how did you even learn of the call?"

"Fuck Caruso, we're the FBI. We have hundreds of analysts and lots of spy hardware."

"I don't recall signing off on any of this."

"You didn't. I did, and there are lots of low-tech ways to do it. The only thing we know is that the burner phone is inside the Griffin house."

Caruso may have tried hard to hide it, but there was no doubt he was concerned about something. Stone took that as further evidence that he knew something about that call. Thank goodness he had not put up the map Chase had made showing the FBI office.

"So, you have diddly squat," Caruso said as he tried to recover.

"Far from it, we're on to something; we just need to back it up."

"Who is 'we,' Stone?"

Stone didn't answer and kept walking.

Caruso barked, "Stone, I asked you a question."

Stone stopped and swung around. Without a change of expression, he said boldly, "Sweating, Caruso?" and walked away.

Caruso heard the words but wasn't sure what they meant. But why would he say those exact words? Did he know the call came here?

He had tried to catch himself, but Stone may have seen a reaction, even if just for a second. As Stone walked away, he had a very strong feeling his boss was involved. Maybe not the murder, but something else related to the case. He just didn't know what.

For his part, Caruso went into his office and used his personal cell phone to call another cell phone. It rang several times, but there was no answer.

Five minutes later, the same number called back.

"You had better have a good reason to break protocol and use this number."

"They triangulated the prepaid phone to the house. They know it called Cartwright, and they think it called here, but they can't prove this location. Destroy the phone and get another and never use it more than once. That is why they call them burner phones! The second item is that Stone is on to something but won't say what it is. It's time to send him back to his home agency down south."

"That is not your decision. And it is too late for that; he knows far too much."

"Well, you can't kill him."

"We can and you may have to do it. We'll get back to you." And the call ended before Caruso could object or even remind her he had not signed up for that.

Chapter 29

Fortitude Security, Kalispell

Alex was back on the dark web. She had really wanted to get in touch with the hacker, but she would never do that without approval from Chase. Smiling, she clicked into several places, some for fun, some for insurance, but most for background. Her brain just recalled these places and someday, she might need to go there.

She had just loaded up the TOR bulletin board when she saw an odd message posted there. It only said: "Cayman Hacker, are you there?"

Alex dismissed it at first, but then wondered if this was the Missoula hacker or a Trinity employee trying to find her. She should have asked Chase, but felt TOR was safe enough to investigate further. It took an hour to make sure all her electronic shields were in place to mask where she really was when she typed in: "What do you want?"

She was shocked when a message came back minutes later: "Have info, need help."

Alex responded: "Where can we meet?"

"Nowhere is safe. I cannot travel."

"How about TOR Mega Chat in one hour?"

"Fifteen minutes."

"Okay."

Before Alex could call, she had to get approval, so she went to the boss's office, although he wasn't there. Maggie, his assistant, said he had gone outside, so Alex went downstairs and out of the building, looking in every direction, but didn't see him. In the back of the property, she saw him talking to Manny by the stables and took off towards him.

Chase saw her coming and stopped Manny mid-sentence as she ran up. "Hey Alex, what's up?"

"She contacted me."

"Who?"

"I think it's the hacker that got into the Missoula forensic files."

"How do you know it's her?"

"I don't know for sure, but I think it is."

"On TOR?"

"Yes."

"You're protected?"

"Of course."

He contemplated the risk and then said, "See what she wants, but be careful. This could be a trap, Alex."

Alex nodded and then ran back to the office just in time to log in as the window opened. Whatever image she had created in her mind for the hacker, this was not it. The face of the girl on the screen was just a slightly older version of herself.

"Hello, I'm Alex."

"I'm Alycia, and I'm not very good at all this dark web stuff, so bear with me."

"Alycia as in, Alycia Gomes?"

"Yes, how do you know of me?"

"Not important. What do you want to know?"

"Is this safe? They say it is, but I need to hear it from you."

"Nothing is perfectly safe, Alycia, but this is pretty darn safe."

"They will kill me if not."

"I understand, let's try something else that is text only," as she wrote another address on a pad of paper and held it up for Alycia to see. When Alycia had written it down, Alex hung up.

The reply in the form of a text came from Alycia several minutes later: "What is this place?"

"It's my own personal chat box. Nobody can get in here."

Alycia had typed back: "Thank you. What is this all about?"

Alex replied: "I was hoping you could tell me?"

There was a pause when Alycia typed: "I'm not really sure. There is something secretive about Trinity files involving clients codenamed 'Phoenix.' Whatever it is, nobody is supposed to know about it."

Alex replied: "I don't understand; you created the files. I saw them."

Alycia typed: "Whatever it is, it is not in the files you saw, but maybe the ones archived here at the firm. But if I try to access them, I'm good as dead."

Alex was more nervous now but replied: "Understand. Grab a paper and pencil."

"Why?"

"I'll need some info from you, but I can help. Check this room daily. We only communicate here. I mean it. Only here."

"Okay. I'm scared. They know someone hacked into Trinity."

"I know, but don't worry, they can't find me. Do not access the files, and you'll be fine."

Alex met with Eddy, and they went about a plan of how to get into the archives of Cartwright and Cartwright without getting caught.

Alex talked to Chase's office thirty minutes later and explained. "So, I had it all wrong. It wasn't the hacker trying to find me, it was the attorney at Cartwright that signed the documents, Alycia Gomes."

"I recall the name. Why would she contact us?"

"The FBI has contacted her twice, and she didn't say it, but I suspect this Decco guy found out, or she told him herself. She wants to understand why she is in danger and thinks the answer is in the archived files in Miami. If she accesses the files, she is dead, so what I thought was, what if I get into their archives and get the files instead?"

"Alex, I believe in you, I really do, but this is all getting out of hand. If you are identified, then the target is on your back. They are clearly watching her, so if they find out she has the files, she's dead before we get the intel. I need to discuss this with Jenkins and maybe even Stone before I can allow it."

"Okay," Alex said, clearly disappointed, and she started to leave.

"Alex?" Chase said.

"Yeah."

"Thank you for always discussing things you could do but running them past me first. I know I can be frustrating, but in a business that is built on trust, doing the right thing means a lot. You're a great employee, and if I get protective, know it is because you mean a lot to me as a person and a colleague."

"I know that. I just feel that Alycia Gomes is trying to do the right thing, and, in her case, she's risking her life to do it."

"Alex, thinking you're letting her down is a worthless gesture if you are both killed."

Alex nodded, but it wasn't clear if she bought that completely.

Chapter 30

Cartwright & Cartwright, Miami

The call from Kalispell ended as Bernard Decco methodically placed the handset of his phone back in its cradle. Despite his past and the fact that such decision making was his job, it was clear this whole affair was getting out of hand. The call from Montana had cemented the fact that the original planning had missed a critical factor.

They had clearly underestimated Agent Stone, especially his two sidekicks, Richard Chase and Billy Jenkins.

Decco and his small team had seemingly planned for every contingency and labored to premeditate how Stone would approach the case. They even factored in the Kalispell Sheriff's involvement. He was not without skill, but at the same time, he wasn't a seasoned detective, but rather the town's steady hand.

But Fortitude Security had not even been mentioned in the original analysis That, even though they seemed to have set the cadence of activity for the last five days.

The recommendation he just received was to eliminate Special Agent Stone, but from his perspective, that was a problem that, once solved, would only bring about an even larger one. With the Police or the FBI, if you harmed one, the other ten thousand came looking for you.

Of course, if need be, a flawlessly executed accident could work, and he would not rule it out. But in the back of his mind, he didn't think Stone had anything, meaning their contact in Kalispell was overreacting. In fact, he suspected the only thing Stone likely had was a suspicion that it was Caruso who received the call and would, therefore, link him to Cartwright. Sloppy business all around for letting a couple of cowboys link the calls, but they had.

Thankfully, in the grand scheme of things, no one person had all the pieces, so for now, nobody had to die as Decco rose from his chair.

The smoking gun in this event was not a person, but rather the archived files themselves.

William and Randle Cartwright were both ambitious men on every front. Brilliant, they were politically astute and well connected. Both had made a name for themselves, handcrafting some of the most complex legal maneuvers in the industry relative to wealth management. Powerfully rich, William was the business executive of the two, and Randle was the one who implemented things, including making sure obstacles in their path were dealt with. Both could accept being slowed down in their many ambitions, but neither tolerated derailment.

Decco reported directly to Randle and was headed for his office now. He had little choice but to escalate this. Despite his brawn, Decco was a consummate planner and systems thinker. His mind easily broke complex tasks into bite-size pieces while simultaneously being able to see and manage them all.

While Randle Cartwright might be capable of such detail, like any seasoned executive of a large and complex organization, he was constantly stuck in a forward gear. He might pause and use his rearview mirror occasionally, but he was forever moving forward. The consequence for Decco was that he could become unstable when you attempted to take him back in time.

When they had discussed the issue a year before, it had not been a problem yet, merely a possibility. But just because it could be a problem, Decco had created a solution. And as far as Randle Cartwright was concerned, that was ancient history. To re-approach him was going to be a mild hit to Decco's reputation and independence, but it was doubtful Randle would overreact.

Unfortunately, the walk to his office proved to be a waste of time. He was traveling, but his assistant would leave a message.

Montana nights were downright cold now, and Chase had considered bringing the fire inside but decided against it. After doing homework with Nate for an hour, he put him to bed and then cleaned up the kitchen after cooking some venison medallions. Chase wasn't much of a hunter himself, but such gamey meats were readily available in town, and venison was one of Nate's favorites.

Out on the patio, he waited for Agent Stone and Jenkins to arrive and started a fire. He had used pine and would add a hardwood once the fire got hot enough. As he lit the fire, he laughed. Nights out by the fire had always been his solitude, his way of thinking. Now, he actually looked forward to chatting it up with the guys about the case.

They both arrived within the hour, and each grabbed a beer as they sat down around the firepit.

Stone spoke first. "I have Caruso on the mat. He saw the evidence board regarding the second call from the burner phone. I played with him a little, saying the call went to our area but that we could not pinpoint it. He was shocked we found it, but it was enough to register a brief panic on his face. Sorry to say it, but I think you guys were right. I'm going to have to watch my back."

"Need any help?" Jenkins asked.

"No, I'll just have to be paranoid for a while," Stone replied as Jenkins and Chase nodded in understanding. They had all been in a similar position before.

Chase went next. "My team may have found a link between Caruso and Cartwright in the capacity of an informant or enforcer. There were two cases over the last three years in which he was the lead agent, and Cartwright was the defendant's law firm. One went to trial in 1997, ending in an acquittal, although it was not obvious that Caruso played a role in the judgment. It could be that he didn't, or that he was that good. The second case is unresolved and ongoing, but it's moving at a snail's pace. The reason is the plaintiff's attorney was killed in a car accident, and the judge stepped down suddenly for undisclosed health reasons."

Both Stone and Jenkins looked up as that description screamed of Cartwright's modus operandi.

"So, nothing to incriminate him, but nothing to exonerate him, either," Jenkins replied.

"Pretty much. But we have a new wrinkle, and I need to air this out to see what you guys think." Chase then recapped the Trinity files, the two attorneys named, and that one, Alycia Gomes, was trying to contact them.

"What do we know of her? My first thought is she has been ordered by Decco to confirm it was Fortitude and then he'll kill your analyst," Stone said.

Chase replied, "That was my first thought as well, but we know from Stone's agent that while Gomes would not provide information, she was clearly doing so out of fear. She also acknowledged that if she went after the files, she was dead. For that reason, this could be legitimate."

"Since she and your analyst would be an immediate risk, what information could this attorney have that is worth it?" Jenkins replied.

"She claims that, unlike the Trinity files from the Caymans, the archived files at Cartwright in Miami show the potential secrets that are behind all this. It has something to do with the clients whose codename is Phoenix, and she thinks Decco is watching her to see if she tries to access the files. Under that threat, she gave us the information necessary to hack in so we could get the files for her."

"Smells like a trap," Jenkins said without a second thought.

Stone said nothing, and after a long pause, Chase asked, "What about you, Stone?"

"I agree it could be a trap, but I can get Agent Williamson to shadow Alycia Gomes, and Chase and his team shadow Alex. We might be able to protect them and bust this open."

Chase thought of Stone's words.

"How about a counterproposal? We go in and get the files but do not involve Alycia Gomes at all, and initially, we don't even let her know we have them. Meanwhile, we'll all play a role in protecting my team. My guess is once we have the files, we won't need an attorney to figure out the missing information."

They all nodded.

Chapter 31

Fortitude Security, Kalispell, Day Six

Chase had assembled the entire team. Alex and Eddy would brainstorm on how to get the files, but first, the entire team was tasked with making damn sure this could not come back to Fortitude. There was little doubt in anyone's mind that Cartwright would try to find who had got in. Having proven themselves before, this would be their only real insurance to not get killed.

While the small team strategized to determine the most bulletproof method to hide who they were and where they were, Chase called in his team from the field. Weston Murray, Gabriel Clarke, and Manny Rojas would arrive in the next twenty-four hours. These former SEALs were guys Richard had either led or fought alongside, and they would join him, Jenkins, and Manny Vasquez. Together, they would protect the Fortitude team.

It was just before eleven when Eddy and Alex entered Eddy's office and closed the door, signaling that the game had begun.

Less than an hour passed before they were able to get into the Cartwright server, but the files they needed were elsewhere. Although they were unaware if the team in Miami could see their attempt and was blocking them at each step, it certainly felt that way. Every attempt they made was seemingly met by a new firewall. If you got through one, you were immediately challenged by another.

Two hours later, they felt as though they had only moved an inch on an endless journey, unsure if they were close or impossibly far away.

It was a quarter past two when Eddy finally got in. The name on the Trinity files had not been Bartholomew but rather the single word Phoenix, so they looked for files under that heading. They found them, but another firewall was in place. Apparently, only certain people could access these files.

"I have never seen such an elaborate security structure in my life. Shit, these guys make the NSA look like amateurs," Eddy said as he typed away.

Alex was doubling the effort and replied with hope. "This is crazy, but we've gotten this far. We have to keep going."

"They must have seen us by now. I'm throwing everything I have at them, but have no idea if it is working."

"Eddy, it must be. Otherwise, they would have thrown us off."

"Valid point, but they could also be letting us stay here while they use the time to locate us."

"I have faith in our defenses. Keep at it."

Upstairs, Chase had left them alone, knowing this would not be an easy hunt, but at the same time, curiosity was killing him. He had done all the busy work he could think of and sat down to read the daily news. He made it through two articles when he went outside to find Manny. Anything was better than waiting.

Meanwhile, Eddy and Alex continued to work as fast as they could to get the files and then get out. This last challenge had proven to be the hardest, and for some time, Eddy honestly thought they might not be able to break it when suddenly they did.

Alex squealed as the file folder opened, and they immediately downloaded the files onto her computer. No sooner had the files downloaded than she quickly opened each file to verify they were readable files. Eddy then closed the electronic door to the Cartwright server. They were out.

Looking at the clock, they had been on the Cartwright & Cartwright server for over five hours.

In Miami, Decco sat in his office, waiting to hear from Randle Cartwright. His private plane had landed just after one that afternoon, but he was meeting someone for lunch and would be back in the office around four. Decco wasn't happy to have waited an entire afternoon. Feeling this was important, he thought perhaps he should just destroy the files. He could always use the meeting to tell Randle what he had done, like asking forgiveness rather than permission.

As the clock moved past four-thirty, Decco's phone suddenly rang, and assuming it was him, he answered.

It was only his assistant. "Mr. Decco, Mr. Cartwright has been delayed and asked me to inform you he'll meet you in his office at 5:15."

"Yes, of course, thanks." Decco hung up, shaking his head. Enough screwing around, he thought, as he rose and walked out of his office toward the elevator. There, he went down three floors to the IT room, which few had access, and went to find the IT Director, Rupert Charleston.

As he entered his office, Charleston jumped, not used to seeing him, thinking something must have happened for Decco to be here. He, like most employees, knew Decco, but didn't want to be confronted by him.

"What has happened?" Charleston asked.

"Why do you think something has happened?"

"It's not like you come to IT for pleasantries, Mr. Decco."

Decco smiled. "You are correct, and this visit is no exception. I need you to delete these files," and handed him a folded piece of paper.

Reading it, Charleston asked, "Might I ask the reason?"

"No. You may not."

Frowning, he considered his next words carefully. "I am sorry, but these are Phoenix files, Mr. Decco."

"I am aware of that. Based on recent events, these six files pose a significant risk and must be destroyed."

Decco observed the expression on Charleston's face. He knew he was weighing the protocols that had been placed on the Phoenix files versus the verbal abuse he was about to receive.

"I mean no disrespect, but I am simply not authorized to delete these files."

"Fine, I meet with Randle in thirty-one minutes," looking at his watch, a vintage 1969 Tag Heuer Monaco. Heading to the door he said, "I'll tell him it is not yet done."

And without another word, Decco walked out. Charleston sat for a few minutes, not wishing to be on either man's bad side. If Decco was meeting Randle Cartwright, then he allowed this, so he would do it.

Chapter 32

Cartwright & Cartwright, Miami

At five thirty-one, Decco entered the opulent office of Randle Cartwright within the Miami Tower complex. One and a half stories tall, this room had a corner view toward Biscayne Bay and was larger than his brother's office by a thousand square feet. Tastefully modern, no expense had been spared in its accouterments, from the Natuzzi sofas and chairs to the handmade desks and tables. The sum of its many styles, colors, and textures showed the talented hand of a world-class designer and a price to match.

Cartwright was sitting in a beautiful cream hued glove leather chair, enjoying a glass of wine, when Decco walked in. Glancing up, he asked, "Bernard, may I interest you in a glass of wine."

"Thank you, but I think I'll have a bourbon," he said as he went to the table and poured an inch of the dark, exotic liquid into a baccarat tumbler. He had been to this office many times and appreciated its finer things such as this Pappy Van Winkle, twenty-three-year-old Family Reserve.

"A stressful day?" Cartwright inquired.

"No more than usual. Thanks for seeing me," Decco walked over and sat down across from him.

"What can I do for you? I have twenty minutes before a meeting with a potential client."

Decco took a sip of bourdon and said casually, "I need nothing from you, but wanted to let you know about an issue. Six files related to a Phoenix project at Trinity have become the heartbeat of an FBI probe. There is no risk from the FBI per se, but the files themselves create undue concern. I received intel to suggest a breach will be attempted soon and to avoid that, I have destroyed them."

"You have destroyed them?" Randle said as if to question him.

"Well, no. I have asked Charleston to destroy them."

"You have overstepped Bernard."

"Randle, I eliminated a threat, nothing more, nothing less."

"A threat created by failures of your own doing. I am aware of the Senator's death."

"Another calculated risk."

"If you say so, but there are many reasons to hold on to the Phoenix files, as that chapter in our story represents both risk and opportunity. As I recall, you do not have the authority to destroy them," he said with a chuckle and took a sip of his wine.

Without more thought, Decco acquiesced, saying, "Very well, I'll tell Charleston to hold off, but their existence is a serious threat."

"Fine, you may use my phone. When you are done, I have a more urgent matter to discuss in our remaining time."

Decco couldn't imagine anything more pressing, but was pleased he had only received a slap on the wrist. He picked up the phone and dialed, and Charleston answered immediately, thinking it was Randle Cartwright himself.

"Mr. Cartwright, how may I help you."

"It's Decco. I'm calling from his office. Hold off on the deletion."

"What? I mean, it is already done, but we have a much larger problem."

"What?"

"Someone accessed the files from outside the firm."

"Shit, I knew it. Who?"

"We're trying to find out."

"When?"

"Earlier today, this morning, we think."

"Find out. Call me when you do."

"Yes, Mr. Decco."

Decco hung up and went back to the corner where Cartwright sat, reaching down to get his drink, said happily, "Done. How can I help you?"

Randle smiled, and they began to discuss another matter.

It was close to ten that same evening when Decco finally returned to the IT floor and met Charleston, who had just called. Both were tired when Decco asked the obvious. "What do we know?"

"By all accounts, the hackers were Russian, and they were on our server for about five hours."

"How does that even fucking happen?"

"They are quite skilled."

"Don't you have alarms and safety features?"

"Of course, but they were clever. They entered as if they were an employee of the firm."

"How in the hell did they do that?" Decco yelled.

"That's the thing. I mean, it's possible, but it would take days, not five hours. It is as if they knew our network."

"How?"

"I really don't know. If this had been going on for a while, I could understand. But in five hours? No way. Either somebody here gave them needed information, or the hacker is one of our own employees."

Decco was about ready to snap, but he would deal with that problem later.

"Did they remove files or just look at files?" Decco asked.

"They do not appear to have opened any files, but they downloaded them. To do so, they even created an approval program to give themselves the permissions."

"Which files did they take?"

"The exact ones you asked me to delete," he said with concern.

"Damnit, I fucking knew it. I'll need a copy of those files to assess what they have."

"Mr. Decco, they aren't here. I have since deleted them, and obviously, I should have done so when you asked."

"Fine, get them from a backup, and I'll get authorization from Cartwright to view them."

"I can't do that."

"Just fucking do it. This is not a game," Decco yelled.

Charleston snapped. "I know, damn it. But when someone like you comes in here and says you and Mr. Cartwright want them destroyed, I did so personally in all variants and made them disappear. That is what 'destroy' means. They are fucking gone."

"So, no way to recreate them," Decco said softly to defuse the situation.

"Well, yes, there are firms that specialize in getting back deleted files, but we would need one we trust."

"And they could really do this?"

"Off the main server, no, but on a backup server, possibly. When a file is deleted, the first letter of the valid filename is replaced with an alpha character, such as a dollar sign. Such a character is not allowed in a valid filename structure, which makes it unretrievable. The information in the file still lives on the disk until the computer overwrites that area with new information. I have secured the backup, so it is not yet overwritten."

"So, if I could find someone, we can get it back."

"Most likely. Is Mr. Cartwright angry?"

"Don't worry about him, worry about me," Decco barked and left in haste. Until a few minutes ago, he had intended to go home and get some sleep, but not now, and he returned to his office.

Chapter 33

North Miami, Florida

After an evening of excessive drinking, Janice Hayward had mildly passed out on her couch an hour before when she suddenly awoke. It took a few seconds before she connected the song *Deceiver* by the band Disturbed to her phone ring tone. She rolled over and grabbed it, hoping it was the wrong number, but no such luck.

"I have a job for you," the scrambled computerized voice said, forcing Janice to snap out of it to understand the words. This was the client that paid really well.

"What do you need?" she asked.

"I need to trace someone from their home network."

"Sure. Name of the user?"

"Alycia Gomes."

"Address?" He provided it.

"Do you know the network name?"

"No."

"Once I get in, what do you want to know?"

"I want to know if she is communicating with an IP address in Kalispell, Montana, and if she has been on the dark web. Two grand up front, and there is another three if you can tell me where on the dark web."

"When do you need it?" she said, thinking, Kalispell again. This was related to her previous job.

"Now."

"It's fucking midnight, dude," she said with a chuckle.

The computerized voice did not appreciate the comment, saying bluntly, "I'll get someone else."

"No, no, chill. I'll do it and text once I have something. It might be quick, but it might take a while if I have to monitor the feed to get answers."

"Understood."

Decco clicked off, hoping he was wrong, although it seemed rather intuitive that the young attorney had just done something very stupid.

It was late in Kalispell as well when Eddy and Alex started to review the entire set of documents, some of which were massive. In total, there were over seven thousand pages of information. Most were contracts, but some were letters, legal briefs and even a few that contained texts and emails. The only thing for certain was that they were going to have to review every page, to determine what information could tie all this together.

Alex had wanted to get this into everyone's hands to speed up the process, but Chase wanted them to limit the number of people who saw the documents. For that reason, only she and Eddy were tasked with the detailed process.

They had gone to their respective workstations as they began to open each file and read them word by word. Alex had also logged into her messaging room on the dark web, leaving it open so she could see if Alycia Gomes had contacted her.

An hour went by when a message popped up, and she read it.

It was short and sweet. Alycia had typed: "Any news?"

Alex replied: "Working on it."

"Wasn't sure. I can barely function. So scared."

"Alycia, what computer do you use to access this room?"

"My own from home. I have my own private network." Alycia typed.

"Okay, be really careful."

"Why, what happened?"

"Alycia, if I can get in, everything will get serious, really fast. We just have to be careful."

"Okay, I understand."

Alex wasn't sure why Chase had been adamant that he didn't want Alycia to know they already had the documents. But if he said it, it was because he had reason to do so. She clicked off the screen and went back to the stack of pages she had been reviewing.

Back in North Miami, Janice was laughing at the easy money she was about to make, even seriously buzzed. She had looked up the woman's address, determined the building and quickly found the building's network and got in to retrieve the credentials for Alycia Gomes. It had taken less than ten minutes.

She followed her feed through the network, and there had been significant use over the last few days. Most were crap, as the girl was shopping for shoes and kitchen appliances. Other history was various news feeds and a great deal of time spent on her work email. Janice looked quickly at some of the content and concluded Gomes was a lawyer. The legalese stuff was making her brain hurt, so enough of that.

Using a memory stick, Janice placed it onto her computer and accessed a quick program to look for anything sent or received from Kalispell. Nothing. Some networks allowed unlimited history, others dropped off everything after a month, which is what this one did. But it didn't matter, even a month back nothing had come in, or gone out, relative to an IP address in Kalispell, Montana.

Next, she began looking to see if she had been on the dark web. She had doubted there was anything, but soon discovered she was wrong. Not only had Gomes been on the dark web, but she had been there earlier that same evening.

While the term *Dark Web* is synonymous with criminals, most people are unaware of the only real difference. On the regular internet, a search is accomplished by using structured domain server names, like dot.com, dot.org, dot.net, etc. and routing address systems like, http:// or the encrypted version, https://.

The dark web uses none of that. Instead, it uses its own version and anything goes. This makes it difficult, if not impossible, to trace something back to the source because the path there is whatever you want it to be. But for an extra three grand, she was going to try.

But two hours later, she had nothing. Tired, Janice texted the contact and told him she had found no evidence of connections to Kalispell, but there was evidence that she had been on the dark web. She would keep trying to find a location, and after sending the text, she let the program run and fell back asleep.

When she woke up five hours later with a massive headache, she got up and checked the program. Nothing. Whoever had set up the location was good, and she had no way of seeing it.

Chapter 34

Gomes Residence, Miami, Day Seven

Alycia Gomes woke at five-forty-five the next morning, a bit earlier than usual, and immediately noticed something was off. Her apartment was very warm and humid, but stranger than that, there were no sounds. It was pure silence, and it took her brain a moment to realize she had no power and, thus, no air conditioning.

Without a concern, she grabbed the workout clothes she had pulled out the night before and changed in the semi-darkness. It wasn't often she lost power here, but there must have been a storm last night. As she walked out of her warm, stuffy apartment into the hallway, it was significantly cooler.

Although she didn't do it every day, Alycia often used the stairs as a self-workout. Since the power was out, her sleepy mind reasoned the elevator was probably down as well, so she headed for the stairs.

She was almost there when she realized the hall lights were on, which triggered her acknowledgment that it was cooler because the air conditioning here was working. Power was out in her apartment, but not here in the hallway.

Not wanting to be late for her Zumba class, she returned to the elevator and sure enough; the lights were active, so she pressed the down button. Happy to hear the sound of its motors, she walked into the elevator car and hit the first-floor button. Exiting into the lobby, she looked both ways, but didn't see anyone else, and headed out the revolving doors to the street.

Her first glance brought confusion. The ground was bone dry with no sign of rain, which made little sense. If the storm was powerful enough to take out her power, it should have left its presence. She made a mental note to call the building maintenance to get her power turned back on after her class.

More alert now to the confusing morning, she started off in a slow jog to get her muscles warmed up and headed to her gym. Minutes later, she was almost there when a tall, wiry man with a poorly shaped beard jumped out of a service way right in front of her.

It all happened so fast, the sudden movement shocked her as she yelped and instinctively put her hands out in front of her. With no additional time to react, she slammed into the man, knocking him to the ground. He was much taller than her but so skinny, Alycia probably outweighed him.

As he fell, she stopped and stumbled, but kept her balance, only to scream. The knife he had been holding in his left hand flew out of his grip and clanked across the concrete as he hit the sidewalk.

With no other thought, Alycia immediately took off in the opposite direction, running for her life. The guy behind her picked up the knife and ran after her, although she was much too fast as she dodged between streets, using anything she could as cover. As she ran, frightened and now thoroughly pissed off, it hit her.

A Cartwright goon had shut off her power to force her down the stairs. They were going to kill her there, and when that didn't happen, the guy she was running from must have been their backup plan.

Still running, tears streamed out of her eyes as she knew she couldn't go back to her apartment to get her car keys in the bowl on the credenza. All she could think of was what people did in movies when they were off the grid. No credit cards, no traceable car, and no cell phone.

Thank God she had grabbed her travel purse and put it in her backpack when she left. She immediately stopped and turned off her phone as she scanned the surrounding grounds. Finding a toothpick on the ground, she used it to open the slot and remove her SIM card. Next, she dashed across the street to a Wells Fargo bank and removed the maximum amount of cash allowed before waving down a taxi.

She had to get the hell out of there. The cab she hailed stopped at the curb. "Where to?" the driver said half asleep.

"The city of Homestead, please."

"That's quite a way from here. You have money?" He said, probably thinking she was going to stiff him. Homestead was some forty miles south of Miami.

"I just got cash," she said, pointing back to the ATM. "I'm late for an appointment, so please hurry," as she jumped in and slouched down in the seat. The driver noticed and figured she was running from an asshole boyfriend. He had seen that look before, frightened and alone.

Arriving in Homestead forty-five minutes later, she paid the fare in cash, exited the cab, and went to a twenty-four-hour convenience store. There, she purchased a prepaid phone. Her initial thought was to call Enrique when she realized they were likely watching him, too. What was she going to do?

It was then that her mind went to the mystery girl, Alex, and she asked the clerk to tell her where the nearest internet kiosk was. After walking there, she wasn't surprised to find they weren't open yet and would not be for another hour.

Once inside, she bought a half hour of computer time and went to the special room that Alex had set up. As she did, she scanned the room and the street for any signs of someone after her.

She frantically typed: "They found out and tried to kill me. I'm in Homestead, Florida, and I don't know what to do. Can you help me? Please!"

To conserve her cash, she went offline and left the kiosk, going to a park across the street before returning an hour later. She logged in to see her only lifeline of hope that morning.

Alex had typed back: "Coming for you. Stay in the area. Hide. Get a prepaid phone."

"I did." And she typed in the number for the phone.

"Okay, it will be a while before I can call you again. Stay hidden the best you can." Alex signed off and nervously looked at the time. Chase would not be in yet, but she knew where he was.

Going outside, she realized she should have grabbed a coat as she ran to the horse stalls, freezing the entire way, and saw him having a coffee with Manny. It was their morning thing.

Manny, in turn, saw her running towards them and told Chase, "Incoming boss."

Richard turned, saw Alex's red, contorted face, and knew something had happened and as she ran into the stable, he grabbed her, "What happened?"

"They just tried to kill Alycia. She's hiding in Homestead, Florida, south of Miami. She has a prepaid phone and hasn't used her credit cards or her phone. Can we go get her?"

"And bring her here?" he asked.

"They'll kill her. You know they will."

He did and turned to Manny. "Manny, tell Nate what happened. We'll be home later tonight. Watch him like a hawk."

Manny didn't skip a beat. "You got it. Go get her."

Without much thought, Chase drove Alex to the nearby Glacier Airport around the side where the private hangers were. He screeched to a stop in front of a large hangar Fortitude had once used as a temporary location when the barn got blown up. In the time they spent there, he got to know the man who flew the plane that was now parked inside.

Richard and Alex both jumped out and headed inside. William (Will) Ketchum wasn't a large man, but he looked more like a boxer than a private pilot. He saw them run in and set down the rag he was using to wipe down the Lear Citation Ultra business jet.

"Hey, Rich, a little early to be moving that fast."

"Ketchum, we have an emergency. Can you fly us to Miami Homestead General Aviation Airport? It's an out-and-back with one passenger returning with us. She's a lawyer, and someone is trying to kill her."

"Hell man, you know this isn't my plane, I just fly the damn thing."

"I know that and will pay whatever the owner wants. I also know if anyone can talk him into it, that would be you."

Ketchum laughed, "You might be right there. Listen, for you, I'll call him, but no guarantees."

Thankfully, the owner was an early riser. Despite his concern about picking up a passenger that someone was trying to kill, Ketchum got approval if Fortitude paid for the cost of the flight. Richard assumed that meant the cost of fuel and would not be cheap. But he wasn't overly concerned. It would come back to him someday if he could save the young girl's life.

It took another forty minutes to log the flight plan and get the plane ready, but they were soon being whisked at 500 miles per hour toward Florida. That was thanks to Ketchum, who was ignoring all rules of practical gas conservation. After a refueling stop in Wichita, they landed in Homestead almost four and a half hours after they had left Kalispell. Ketchum took care of the third round of fuel as Richard and Alex headed inside the small FBO terminal.

Alex had called Alycia on her prepaid phone thirty minutes before and told her to take a taxi to this small general aviation airport on Avenue 225. As she walked toward the terminal, she realized she had only seen Alycia for a second on the video chat and wasn't sure if she would recognize her. Once inside, she knew that wouldn't be an issue. Not only wasn't she there, but neither was anyone else. A solitary clerk was in the corner, and Alex went to his desk. The man turned.

"Can I help you, miss?"

"We just arrived, and we're here to pick up a young woman. Have you seen her?" she said in a panic.

"What does she look like?"

"We have not met, but she's under thirty, has brown hair, and is a few inches shorter than me."

"Nope, nobody like that," he replied having noticed the private jet, wondering who the heck these people were. They looked more like farmers than millionaires.

Watching the scene in front of him, Richard was thinking of how they could locate Alycia if she didn't show up and now wished he had left Alex at home.

As if to answer his concern, the man at the desk smiled and said, "I see a taxi heading this way. Maybe that's her."

Alex ran outside and no sooner had the taxi stopped, Alycia saw her and burst into tears, as she jumped out of the cab and ran to her. She was still dressed in her workout clothes, but at that moment, nobody cared. Richard came out and while the two girls embraced, he paid the driver, looking in every direction as if expecting company.

The driver, in turn, saw the private jet and realized he should have charged three times the amount until he saw the outline of a gun in Richard's rear holster. That made him want to leave right then, which he did.

Chase ushered them inside to wait for the fuel to be delivered. While the girls used the time to make each other feel better, he kept an eye on the expanse of the airfield. Thankfully, nothing happened, and within an hour, they were headed back to Kalispell.

Enrique Alvaro had been at work for close to three hours and had spent the entire time trying to find Alycia. She had not come to work and was not answering her text or calls. It was as if she had turned off her phone, which she never did.

It was a Thursday, and he knew she had a Zumba class earlier that morning. When he called to see if she was there, they said she never showed up and reminded him she would have to pay a late cancellation fee.

Even more concerned now, he knew her apartment wasn't far away, so he made an excuse to get a coffee and rushed there. The doorman knew him and let him up, but when he arrived at her door, nobody answered. He went back downstairs and told him she might be in trouble, and he called security, who opened her door. Nothing seemed amiss other than her unit having no power, and inside the apartment, it was excessively hot and humid. He noted her car keys were in the bowl, so she wasn't there, but she hadn't driven away either as the security guy turned the power back on.

Enrique thanked both for their trouble and talked them out of calling the police. When he finally headed back to the office, he was in a panic and tried to calm himself when his phone rang.

The sound scared the crap out of him, but even more so when the caller ID said it was Bernard Decco.

Oh, fuck he thought, what had Alycia done?

"Hello," he said weakly.

"Mr. Alvaro, it is Bernard Decco."

"Good morning, sir. How can I help you?"

"Were you running?"

"What?"

"You sound out of breath."

"Oh, right. I went for a coffee and ran back when I remembered I had a call."

Decco smiled, knowing he had just been to her apartment. Since her escape early that morning, Decco had two people watching her building.

"I had a question for Alycia. Have you seen her by chance?"

"No, it's weird. She's not in, and she never misses a day of work."

"Strange, yes. If you see or hear from her, have her call me, okay?"

"Yes, of course." Enrique felt sick as he headed for the bathroom, his gut telling him his friend was dead. Why hadn't she listened to him?

After splashing water on his face, he suddenly smiled. She couldn't be dead. Decco had just called. If he was looking for her, that meant something had happened, and she was on the run.

Chapter 35

Chase Residence, Kalispell

The trio arrived back in Kalispell at just after nine that evening, and rather than go to Fortitude, they all went to the cabin. Although Richard had not said it aloud, he was still somewhat mistrustful of Alycia Gomes. Until he could trust her, he didn't want her to see or have immediate access to Fortitude. Especially not the war room where Eddy and Alex had created their own version of the FBI's evidence board, and the documents from Cartwright were all over their offices.

Despite his misgivings, he was a gracious host and quickly introduced her to Nate and Manny. He told her Manny was part of their security detail and that the entire property was surrounded by highly trained warriors. It was true, although only Weston Murray had arrived thus far, but the other two would be there soon enough.

He and Nate made some small bites for everyone, and they all made their way back to the living room, where Chase lit a fire. As he did, Nate handed the girls a blanket, especially Alycia, who was freezing in her yoga pants and sleeveless workout top.

As the girls cuddled their blankets, Chase said, "Sorry about the temperature. We tend to accept what nature gives us out here since the cabin doesn't have a heater or air conditioning."

Alycia was thankful for the blanket and said sincerely, "This is perfect, thank you, and I'm not sure what to say. I owe you my life for getting me out of Miami."

"Thanks to you doing all the right things, it was uneventful. We were just incredibly lucky to get a fast ride down. Glad you're safe," he replied, saying nothing about the five-thousand-dollar fuel bill and another thousand dollars in landing fees.

He had just sat down when the rear slider opened, and Cheyenne Denton walked in with Weston Murray, one of Chase's former SEAL buddies.

Richard smiled and stood. "Well, this is a surprise." Murray laughed and walked over, giving him a firm handshake and waved goodbye to Cheyenne, before heading back out. Weston and Manny had already put together a security rotation for the night.

Walking to Cheyenne, Richard asked, "Look at you up and about already. You look great," as he gave her a small hug, trying not to hit her arm. The dressing on her arm was much smaller, although she still wore an arm sling to avoid flexing. Her head bandage had been replaced by a large gauze pad, and she had removed her ponytail and pulled her hair straight back, stuffing it into her shirt. The head dressing was concealed by a baseball cap.

"More security?" Alycia asked as Murray left, now looking at Cheyenne.

"Yeah, they're all over and just itching for a little action." Manny smiled at the comment, knowing that Chase wanted her to think security was everywhere. That said, he wasn't sure if he was trying to put her at ease or scare the shit out of her.

Cheyenne stood awkwardly when her eyes glanced at Alycia, and Richard said to put her at ease, "Cheyenne, this is Alycia Gomes. Alycia, this is Cheyenne Denton. While she could easily be part of our security detail, she is the lead CSI for the Kalispell Coroner's office." Cheyenne gave a little wave.

"Wow, a CSI. Did you get hurt on the job?" Alycia said with admiration.

"Yeah, you could say that," she said, wondering why the girl was half-dressed. Thinking she might be with Chase, Cheyenne said rather snarkily, "What do you do, Alycia? I don't think I've seen you around here before."

"Gosh, no. I've never even been to Montana. I'm an attorney from Florida, and I'm not even sure my freezer gets this cold."

Chase saw Cheyenne's face tighten and thought it best to bring out the elephant in the room. "Alycia is with Cartwright & Cartwright." As he said it, Alycia looked down, suddenly feeling guilty in this crowd.

Cheyenne barked, "What the hell!" as her left hand balled into a fist, and she almost reached for her Glock.

Alycia jumped back with fear in her eyes and said to Cheyenne, "It's not what you think. They tried to kill me this morning."

"And a few days ago, they killed my dear friend and almost killed me and our security guard. Excuse me if I'm not thrilled to meet you," Cheyenne snapped.

"I know, I know, I'm so sorry, but I am not them. After they tried to kill me, I reached out to Alex, and she and Mr. Chase saved me and brought me here. I promise I'm not part of this and don't really know what is going on."

Cheyenne relaxed her hand and asked suspiciously, "Why would they kill you."

"Ever since the FBI approached me, I've been trying to understand what is going on with a project I was involved in last year. The only answers may be in the archived files in Miami, but I was warned that if I accessed them, they would kill me. I met Alex on the dark web, and she's trying to get the files for me. They must have found out, and now I'm here with nothing but what I'm wearing and can never go back home again."

As the reality of her situation hit her, she started to cry.

Cheyenne may have come on strong and meant it, but she didn't want this and walked over to Alycia who was shaking between sobs, and gave her a one-handed hug.

As she did, she looked over at Alex and Richard, using her facial expression to say she was sorry.

"Alycia, you're in good hands. We'll sort it out. Sorry if I came on strong, but you are working for some nasty people," Cheyenne said.

There was an awkward silence when Alycia replied, "So, who exactly are you guys? I'm grateful, but I don't understand your role in all this?"

Richard said, suddenly serious. "Before we get to that, why don't you go first? How did you get involved with Cartwright & Cartwright?"

Looking down, she understood. She wasn't trusted here.

"After I graduated from Penn State, I went looking for work. We all did. I had heard rumors about Cartwright, but a recruiter for them pursued me and my friend Enrique Alvaro. It was flattering to be wanted, and the money they were offering was twice what we were expecting, so we both talked to them and were accepted. It is a good job, but after a while, it seemed to me we changed a lot of documents. Often, those changes represented potential problems for the firm. But the issues suddenly went away."

"Is that where Bernard Decco comes in?" Richard asked.

"I worked down in the trenches, so I have no idea, but he is certainly the one that seems to handle things from what I see and hear."

"Which brother does Decco work for?"

"Randle. I've been told William is the strategist, and Randle is the one that makes things happen. So, you guys know about Decco?"

"Not really. We learned of him while trying to understand the circumstances around the death of our former Senator," Alex replied.

"Winston Bartholomew," Alycia said softly.

"Yes. As we dug into that, we found other names, other oddities, and several people who were deceased. As you said, each time we thought we had something, it went away through theft, intimidation, or death."

"Are you with the FBI?" Alycia asked.

Richard thought for a moment and answered. "No, we are a private security company working on behalf of the senator's widow, although we interface heavily with the FBI and local law enforcement."

Alycia replied honestly, "The Senator was known as Phoenix, but others have shared that same codename, although I don't know why. I drew up three of his contracts, but there are many of us."

"We know that. Tell me, given his name is not on the contracts, who is the beneficiary?"

"With Phoenix files, there isn't one. The assets go to the Trinity partners on death. I always thought that was kind of strange."

"And the silent partner to Trinity?"

"I don't know him, but he lives in New York, and yes, sometimes payments go to him as well."

"He was murdered five nights ago."

Alycia gasped, and her eyes filled with terror. "Mr. Chase, I don't know you, but I'll give every penny I have if you can protect me. I can't die for this. I'm only twenty-nine!" as she began to cry again. "I didn't do anything wrong; it was just a job. These are all valid contracts and tax shelters."

Richard smiled and softened a tad. "Alycia, nobody here is accusing you. And as far as danger goes, it's not just you. They're after all of us."

"But this is what you do, right? I mean, you guys know how to deal with this."

Alex said it for them, "It's not that we are unphased, but danger is danger. This is far from our first rodeo."

Chase smiled. "Alex, do me a favor. Nate and Alycia are about the same height. Take her to his room, wake him up, and get her some warm clothes. Meanwhile, we'll try to think about the sleeping arrangements."

Alex replied, "Alycia and I can sleep in the attic of Fortitude. Murray is there to stand guard and almost nobody even knows the rooms are up there."

"I can join you," Cheyenne said.

"If you're up to it, the more the merrier," Richard said to Cheyenne. Turning to Alex, he added, "As far as the barn is concerned, it is too isolated, and if they come, that is the first place they would go. No, stay here in the cabin. You girls share my room, and I'll sleep out here."

Soon after, Richard and Manny went out to find Murray, and Alex and Alycia went to Nate's room to get some warm clothes.

Chapter 36

Cartwright & Cartwright, Miami

It was close to eleven that evening when Bernard Decco finally left the office for home. He didn't have to go far since his condo was ten floors above his office in the Miami Tower complex. He entered and without changing, went straight to his bar and made a drink. Sitting in a leather chaise lounge facing the windows, the lights of Miami twinkled below and, as he took the first sip. Could this day have gone any worse?

Someone had the very files he had sought to destroy, and neither Randle nor William Cartwright had a clue about the breach, although they soon would. The person responsible for the hack was unknown, and the facilitator, Alycia Gomes, disappeared. Despite his vast network in Florida, nobody could find her, and she had not accessed her credit cards or phone in the last eighteen hours. It was possible she had used an ATM, but with only four hundred dollars from a single transaction, how far could that get her? She must have been planning this for a while, and he cursed himself for letting himself get soft with her.

She had played him. Despite her outward appearance and mousy demeanor, she had been capable of eluding the first and second attempts at her life. To also have the aptitude to escape and get off the grid with no car and petty cash meant she was being helped by someone. Maybe the FBI?

One thing was for certain, it wasn't her guy friend, Enrique Alvaro. He had been thoroughly questioned and if he knew, he would have spilled his guts. For now, he was being monitored, but otherwise left alone. Decco had no doubt the young man knew the consequences if he even thought to contact her or the FBI.

Frustrated and working to consider the next move, his phone suddenly rang. He intuitively grabbed his cell, but that was not the phone that was ringing. He went to his jacket pocket and removed the burner phone that spoke to their contact in Kalispell.

"Decco."

"I understand you're missing an attorney."

"I'll find her."

"I might be able to help with that," The woman said, bringing a smile to Decco's face.

"That would be much appreciated."

"Look no further than Fortitude Security in Kalispell."

"They have her. How?"

"My source saw the owner, Richard Chase, and a young girl depart on a private jet with a flight plan to Homestead, Florida, early this morning. They arrived back in Kalispell a little while ago with another young woman wearing gym clothes."

"Well, well. How fucking clever," Decco hissed.

"You need to get a handle on this mess, Mr. Decco. The attorney is a problem, but with them, it is worse. I have no idea what she knows, but she might just know enough for them to understand."

Decco gave thought to what she just said, and suddenly, he tensed. Shit, he had missed it completely.

He said out loud, not really wanting her to know.

"It also means the breach into our servers was not Russians but Fortitude Security. Unbelievable, they're working together."

"Breach. What breach? Who is working together?" she screamed.

Realizing he had just screwed up, he replied, "I think it was Fortitude that hacked into our server and took some files relative to a Phoenix project at Trinity."

"So, in addition to our attorney, they also have our files."

"I believe so, yes."

"Decco, you had better end this now, or you alone will bear the consequences. Do the brothers know?"

"Not yet. I was waiting until I had a plan and will bring them up to date in the morning."

"Hold off. It is doubtful you will survive that meeting. Get our files back, eliminate the threats, and then we'll tell them what happened."

The phone hung up as Decco rose, removed the battery and smashed the phone with a meat tenderizer and then took out another burner phone and turned it on.

He smiled. Since he knew he was fucked anyway, killing the bitch on the other end of the phone would be one of his last official acts. But not before Agent Stone. It had to be him who set all this up.

Chapter 37

Chase Residence, Kalispell, Day Eight

Chase woke early and started to make breakfast. He led a simple life, and usually, it was just him and Nate, with an occasional meal with Manny. But this was getting crazy. Between inside and out, there were now nine mouths to feed. To be honest, his small kitchen wasn't set up for this, and he reminded himself that he needed to cater food for the guys outside today. It was better to separate the groups, anyway. Under these circumstances, having them all in one place was unwise.

He was having coffee when Cheyenne came out, and he poured her a cup as she smiled. "I could wake up like this every morning."

Chase blushed and shook his head. "Thanks for helping with Alex and Alycia. Neither is ready for what's coming."

"Are we?" she said bluntly.

"Not yet, but we will be."

"Why isn't the FBI here?"

"Can't share that just yet. But they will be if anything happens. Are you sure you're okay with this?"

"I'm left-handed, so this is awkward, but it won't stop me. I'm good."

Chase nodded and turned the sausage a quarter-turn.

"Thanks for letting me stay," she said more seriously.

Chase looked at the sausage and replied, "Glad to have you." It was her turn to blush.

"I forgot to mention it yesterday, but Abe Kaufman is still hanging in there."

"Jenkins told me the same."

Chase turned the sausage again as Alycia walked in, wearing a pair of Nate's jeans, a baseball cap, and a flannel shirt.

"Morning, guys. Any coffee?"

"Full pot. Cups are in the cabinet above."

She poured a cup, still half asleep, and came over to them. "Smells good. I never eat a proper breakfast."

They both laughed, and Cheyenne replied, "In our jobs, you never know what the day is going to bring, so we always pile up when we can." Alycia noticed how comfortable they were together and assumed they were an item. Lucky girl, she thought. Mr. Chase was ruggedly attractive.

"So," she asked. "I need some help. I mean, my parents must be freaking out, and my friend Enrique likely thinks I'm dead. How can I let them know I'm okay?"

Chase turned the sausage again and said with little room for error. "I'm sorry, Alycia, but you can't. If they were watching you, they were watching Enrique. They have already questioned him, and he'll know they didn't harm you because they are looking for you. As for your parents, they'll be approached next, if not already. If they know, they'll tell. For that reason, they cannot know."

Alycia frowned, and Cheyenne added. "A few more days, and this will all blow up. They can last a few more days."

It wasn't the answer she wanted, but Alycia just nodded.

After breakfast, Chase took off, telling them he'd be back in a few hours, and headed to Sheriff Jenkins station. Jenkins wanted to update him after the brutal review by his command regarding the theft of backup evidence from the Kalispell Coroner's office. Given what had gone down in Missoula, it was hardly the sheriff's fault, but shit rolls downhill as they say. As he walked in,

Stone was there as well, although neither he nor Jenkins looked to be in a very good mood.

"Morning, guys. What happened? Why the long faces?" Chase said.

"Are you serious? We have zip for evidence, and both our respective commanders want our asses."

"We might have more than you think. I have some updates."

"Like what?" Jenkins asked, as if there was anything he could say to change the situation.

"We were able to get the files from Cartwright & Cartwright relative to the Phoenix project, or at least the six files that represent the investments from Winston Bartholomew. As we now understand it, this is a series of Trinity projects that all use the codename Phoenix to hide the identity of the investors. There are many under this heading, not just Bartholomew. We also know that Phoenix projects have no beneficiary. On death, the assets go to the Trinity partners and Matthew Pullman prior to his death."

"And you got this from the files?"

"No. We got that from Alycia Gomes, the Cartwright & Cartwright junior attorney, who is currently having coffee in my cabin."

"What?" Jenkins proclaimed.

"Alex and I went to Miami to rescue her yesterday when Decco's goons tried to kill her. She and Alex are locked up in the cabin with Cheyenne, and three of my guys are monitoring the property."

"Hell yeah. Now we're getting somewhere." Stone said as a smile finally reached his sour-puss face.

"Unfortunately, that news also brings some realities to our situation," Chase said solemnly. "If Decco tried to kill Alycia, it is because they know of the hack and that Alycia provided Alex the network information. Although we don't think they have any idea it was Fortitude, they could have figured it out. And even if they didn't, our coming and going from the airport with a flight plan to Florida may have gotten back to Griffin. If that is true, it would be logical for Cartwright and Griffin to suspect Alycia is here, and Griffin's next call would be Caruso."

Stone smiled. "Fine, let's go over and arrest Griffin right now. It might not stick, but it will buy us two days of freedom."

"We don't even know it's him. It's just his house." Chase replied.

"You still think the wife and Katherine are together."

"Until the evidence says otherwise, we can't rule it out."

"But since we already have the files, can't we just get the secrets and reveal them to the FBI before they can strike," Jenkins said matter-of-factly.

"Although we think the files can blow this open, we don't know that as a fact, and neither does Alycia. But if the files are critical, then they are coming to get them back, and likely in the next twenty-four hours. There are thousands of pages, so there won't likely be enough time before we must defend ourselves. Billy and I have set a security perimeter around my place before, so we'll get a plan together for the property, but I think the situation with Caruso is important."

"If Caruso is involved, he'll never get his hands dirty. It's not his style."

"Think about it, Stone; the only way for him to help Decco is to make sure we cannot stop them. If I were him, I'd arrest us all."

"On what grounds?" Stone said.

"Some trumped-up nonsense; it doesn't matter. You said it yourself about Griffin. It doesn't have to be real or make sense; it just has to stop us for a day or two so they can get their files away from us unmolested."

The gears in Stone's head were rolling in fast circles, and he knew Chase might not be far off the mark. "Fine, let's say you're right. What can we do in one freaking day?"

Jenkins had been thinking of that exact question. "Stone, you need to confront Caruso and let him know what's about to happen. He'll have to know they'll likely kill him after he stops us. But if you can get him to do the right thing, between Chase's team and the local FBI team, we can win this. And then blow up the Cartwright cartel or whatever the hell this is."

"But he'll know he has nothing to lose. Why help me?"

Chase replied to Stone. "I don't know why, but I think he's doing this for money. Once he knows he's next, I think he'll do the right thing. Hell, we can even make it look like he and you two set up this whole thing to break open the case."

Stone looked to the ground, and his face twitched. He put his hands in his pockets and said sincerely, "Okay, I'll do it. Hey, if anything happens, I just wanted to say thanks for everything."

"Jeez, Stone, don't start crying. Just get the hell over there and get Caruso on our side," Jenkins hollered as they all started to laugh.

Chapter 38

FBI Resident Agency, Kalispell

Caruso sat in his office, knowing his new burner phone was going to light up any minute. He had no idea what had happened over the last twenty-four hours, but had heard nothing, which was far more troublesome. The Missoula incident was going to have enormous consequences, and it was just fifteen minutes later when the phone rang. "Caruso," he said with authority, although it wasn't the caller he expected.

"It's Bernard Decco. We have a problem."

Decco explained what had happened with the files and Alycia Gomes, including the fact that they were both in Kalispell.

Caruso replied, "What a disaster. What do you need?"

Decco told him what he expected from him.

"Listen, Decco, I get this is bad, but I'm only paid to slow things down."

"I don't really give a shit what you think. The files and the attorney with Fortitude mean we are just days from them blowing the top off our employer, and if they don't survive this, neither do we. I need you to stop them from accessing the FBI team as an army against us. Arrest them or kill them. I don't care. We need them out of the picture for forty-eight hours. When we come in tomorrow to retrieve the files and retake control of our attorney, we will do so without law enforcement intervention."

"Decco, for Christ's sake, I only have so much power. I can't do that."

"You will do whatever I ask, or you'll be the first person I kill. At this point, I have nothing to lose."

Caruso hesitated. Had that prick just threatened him? Yes, he had. "Fuck you, Decco. Don't you ever threaten me!"

Decco just laughed and said, "You signed up for this, Caruso. Do it or die," and the call ended.

Caruso realized he had been yelling and noticed a few faces looking at him through the glass, hoping they had not heard the words. As if it couldn't get worse, Stone had just walked into the station and was heading for his office.

Stone himself looked like a caged animal about to face his hunter and wasn't sure how it would go. Inside the agency, surrounded by his own team, Caruso wouldn't likely kill him there. At least, he didn't think so as he arrived at his door. Before he could think further, he opened it and closed it behind him.

Caruso barked. "Not now, Stone. The door was closed for a reason."

"We need to talk, Damion."

Stone watched the blood drain out of Caruso's face, knowing then they had already called him, just as Chase had said.

"Make it fast."

"I know about you and Cartwright. I also think Cartwright knows that Fortitude has their files and their attorney, which means they are coming here to get their files back. As I sit here, a SIG P226 is aimed at your balls, so if you make any attempt to kill me, I will kill you first. Further, I also know what they have asked you to do."

"You don't know shit, Stone. Your days as an FBI agent are over. Do you hear me? Fucking over!"

"As are yours, Damion; I'm not the only one with this information. But if you care to hear it, I have a plan to save us both."

"You're in way over your head."

"I suspect we both are, but here it is. You and I have been working together to break up a criminal syndicate within Cartwright & Cartwright that we found while investigating Bartholomew's murder. You even risked your life going undercover to infiltrate their Kalispell-based agent. They are coming to get back their incriminating files, but we're going to stop them. In a few days,

Fortitude will break open the facts, and all the people wishing us dead will flee, take their own lives, or die trying. There won't be anyone in power capable of going after us. We win, the bad guys lose."

At first, Caruso didn't say a word, and Stone couldn't tell if he was thinking about it or determining his next denial. What he said next was unexpected.

"Why in the hell would you help me?"

Stone paused and replied, "I'm only doing so for the greater good."

Caruso let out a deep breath and sighed. "It was never meant to be like this, Stone. I was just paid to slow things down."

"I don't care Damion, those demons belong to you. We have less than twenty-four hours to save ourselves and the lives of many innocent people. They won't stop until they have their files back."

"I know."

"So, are you in?" Stone asked.

Chapter 39

Fortitude Security, Kalispell

It was late afternoon when Chase made his way back over to the barn. Alex had convinced him that Alycia could do more good than bad with their dive into the documents. So, there they were, reviewing each page of the document set. To speed up, they printed the documents.

To her credit, Alycia knew what the boilerplate legal stuff was, allowing them to set aside thousands of pages of contracts and focus on the smaller, detailed pages. But after five hours, they had found nothing.

Chase had joined them and could tell by their faces that they had yet to uncover the secrets of the Phoenix files, so without a word, he just sat down.

"Alycia, if I have this right, Trinity did many deals. Most were legitimate tax shelters and asset management arrangements for high-wealth clients. But occasionally, they did special deals and codenamed those investors as 'Phoenix.' Is that correct?" Chase asked.

"I believe so, yes."

"And these deals contained no beneficiary, only Trinity, if the person expired."

"Yes."

"We know that Winston Bartholomew was a person codenamed Phoenix, and we think he was brought into Trinity by his brother-in-law, Matthew Pullman. He was the ten percent owner living in New York."

"If you say so. I only know of him because of the occasional distributions he received," she replied.

"What we can't figure out is why Bartholomew would enter a deal with Trinity when he knew it was related to Cartwright & Cartwright. The same company he knew was dirty from his time in the Senate?"

Alycia replied. "That is what we are looking for in these files. I mean, not just the Senator, but why would anyone invest in Phoenix projects?"

"And I appreciate that, but we're running out of time. The enemy is on the way, and if we don't have the secret, we'll have to fight the war. Find me the link. Why did Bartholomew invest in Trinity?"

Eddy stiffened. "Listen, Boss, you say it was him making the investment, but couldn't it be the wife? I mean, it was her brother and her money."

"But if she is the real investor, then why did Decco kill the Senator?" Alex asked.

"We don't know that he did, but if she is involved, maybe he was killed because he found out his wife was involved. Since he knew the company was bad, he would certainly object," Eddy replied.

Chase was getting impatient. "Possible, but we're speculating. We believe Griffin is the guy feeding info to Cartwright. If that is true, how does Katherine fit in or even gain from his death? The investments on his death go to Trinity Holdings, not her."

"What if Katherine is one of the Trinity partners?" Eddy said fishing.

"Well, if that is true, then the Kalispell operative for Cartwright is a woman, not Griffin. Hold tight."

Chase walked out for some privacy and called Stone. "Hey, is Caruso on board?"

"Not sure. He acknowledged he was hired to slow things down, meaning the case, but he did not say whether he was in or out."

"We need to know if the voice he spoke to in Kalispell was a woman or a man."

They hung up, and Stone called Caruso, who was standoffish at first but finally said, "A woman."

Caruso had never spoken to Angie Griffin or Katherine Bartholomew, so he had no idea which voice he had spoken to. Stone did not say a word and hung up, calling Chase back.

"Chase, he says it's a woman. He described her as a cold bitch with ice in her veins."

"The real Katherine?" Chase said.

"Possibly."

"Should we just arrest her?"

"With what evidence?" Stone replied.

How screwed up was this that they were about to be attacked from Florida, but they still knew nothing about who was pulling the strings right there in Kalispell?

Chapter 40

Chase Residence, Kalispell, Day Nine

The plan was set, and they had tried to imagine all scenarios. Chase had sent Nate to a neighbor's house on the pretense that he would have to leave for a day, and Manny was unable to watch him. Nate had stayed there before. As an insurance policy, Alex downloaded all the files to a memory stick, with one going to Jenkins, one to Stone, and a third going to Cheyenne. No matter what happened, the information would be vetted in time.

Outside the barn, Richard met Cheyenne. "Listen, I appreciate you wanting to help the girls, but by doing so, you're putting yourself in harm's way," he said honestly.

Smiling, she replied, "I'll take that as you're concerned for me."

"Of course, I am concerned, Cheyenne. These people mean business."

She blushed and pulled up her blouse to reveal her Glock 43. It also revealed a significant wolf tattoo that crept from somewhere lower in her jeans, with only the top of its head peeking above her waist. "Bring it on."

Chase would never forget that view and she saw his surprise. "What do you know of my people?" Referring to the Kalispel Indians.

"I know they considered the Northwest Plateau their tribal lands. And that the upstream people were known as Pend d'Oreille and your people, the downstream people were known as the Kalispel with one 'L.'"

"True. And we, like most indigenous people, consider the wolf to be our spiritual guide. They are teachers of wisdom and act as our protectors. You don't have to worry about me."

"Cheyenne, I know you're tough. I'm just saying this is a situation where they are out to kill us, so we have to kill them first."

"So, you're saying you don't want me there, that only the men are capable of defending themselves," she said with her anger visible across the hard lines of her face.

"I didn't say that at all. I just don't want anything to happen to you. They came close to killing you in Missoula, and this team will be larger and better prepared."

It took her a second before she understood his logic and smiled. "I like you too. My wolf will protect us both."

It was just after four when Jenkins got word that a charter plane had just landed at the Glacier Airport and the men getting off were likely mercenaries. Additional sightings came from local sources who had seen multiple SUVs with sizeable men inside. All were heading to the Chase property.

At the stables next to the cabin, Chase would stay there to confront them while the two former SEALs, Murray, and Rojas held defensive positions. Jenkins and his two deputies were in the forest as snipers. Manny, Clarke and a few of Manny's friends guarded the outside perimeter of the cabin and Fortitude.

The million-dollar question was Stone and Caruso. The six or seven agents would tip the balance of power, but only if they showed up and so far, they were nowhere to be seen.

It was close to seven when the SUVs came down Highway 2 at speed and barely slowed as they drove toward Fortitude. Chase had rigged the entrance, but the explosive charges had missed the first SUV. Thankfully, the second took a hit and jumped a few feet into the air before it burst into flames.

The two SUVs behind it could not get through, so from the highway, they skidded to a stop on the dirt shoulder. Doors opened, and the gunman jumped out, running toward the Fortitude barn as the sheriff snipers tried to stop them.

Behind the Chase property was a mountain that connected this valley to the other side of Kalispell. Someday, Chase hoped to acquire that land, but for now, it was a secondary funnel for bad guys to enter the property. Deputies Thompson and McLoud fired at will, but it was unclear how many made it down the mountainside onto his property.

As Chase suspected, they momentarily only cared for the barn and their files, and all the men they could see seemed to move in that direction.

The ensuing firefight had been expected from Chase and his team, but the bad guys thought they might have easy access. While they took cover, Chase and his team were trying to drive them away from the cabin and toward the barn that housed Fortitude.

From inside the cabin, Cheyenne heard the firefight and was in communication with Weston Murray until he was hit. His last command was that he was down, would be okay, and to contact Rojas if needed.

Cheyenne didn't panic but was highly concerned. To shoot Murray, said something about those coming for them. That concern turned into fear when she couldn't get hold of Rojas on his comm device.

She turned to Alex and Alycia, "Okay, girls, we have a problem," and she explained the situation. Alex was scared but ready, but Alycia was downright terrified.

It had been assumed that the forward teams could slow the incoming while the snipers and Chases' team would point the enemy at the barn. That is not exactly what happened. Many of the incoming forces went to the barn, but it wasn't long before they understood it was empty. A few went in for the files, but it was clear the rest were looking for Alycia. They had orders to get the files and the attorney.

To Cheyenne, seeing this from concealed windows meant they were going to be easy targets when they made it to the cabin. Some wouldn't get that far, but some would, meaning they needed to get out. Heading to the back patio, she led Alex and Alycia there and pulled her Glock. Just before she opened the door, she looked at Alycia.

"Listen, they are going after you first, then Alex. Change clothes with me."

"What?" Alycia asked.

"Take off your clothes. You'll wear mine, and I'll wear yours. They have scoped this out and know who they think you are. You'll both run for the highway. Go past it and don't stop. There is a trail on the other side. Just keep running in that direction."

"Where are you going?" Alex said with worry.

"I'm going to the hills behind us. I've spent my whole life here, and they'll never find me. But they will come because they think I'm Alycia, which should give you both the cover to get across the highway unseen."

Alycia yelped, "Cheyenne, you can't do this for me. I did this. It is all my fault. I'll go, and you two will go for the highway."

"No offense, but you'd be dead in minutes. I can give you cover. Trust me."

After they swapped clothes, Cheyenne opened the door slowly, but nobody was there. Holding her Glock in front of her, they all stepped out.

"Okay, one, two, three. Go." Alex and Alycia took off to the right, while Cheyenne, dressed as Alycia, went to the left.

Chapter 41

Chase Residence, Kalispell

Chase had his hands full while the mercenaries attempted to get past them and head from the barn to the cabin. The snipers were doing their part and picking off targets as they moved in front of the lake, the only way to the cabin from the east. Chase, Murray, and Jenkins were firing as fast as they could load, and the incoming force was down to less than six men. One or two of whom were still in the barn looking for the files.

As the enemy inched forward, they used the natural and artificial cover to make their way toward the cabin. Chase and his team dove for cover and then popped up to fight, trying to keep them from there.

Just minutes later, several SUVs came flying down the highway, skidding to a stop on the road. Lights ablaze, at least a dozen jumped out, fully armed with the highly visible identification on their FBI jackets and hats.

It took just minutes to get the upper hand, and Chase was relieved until he saw Alycia running across the field next to the lake, heading for the mountains.

"Alycia, no. Get the fuck down," Chase said to himself as he took off after her, surprised at how fast she was. Suddenly, there was the sound of a single gunshot, and Alycia went down hard, face first.

Chase stopped in his tracks. His SIG was out, the safety off, as he slowed his breathing and listened. The killer was here, and he was going to die. Without looking, he swapped magazines to ensure he had eighteen chances, slipping the partial one into his belt.

The first shot came over Chase's shoulder as he dropped, but he held on to the SIG with his right hand. He jumped up and fired in the direction the shot had come from.

There was a muted yelp as Chase jumped up and walked slowly towards the sound. As he approached, a dark shape was on the ground, frantically looking for his weapon. Chase held out the SIG and placed the sight on his head from fifty feet away.

"Don't move, or you're dead."

It was dusk, but light enough to tell that the look in the man's eyes was inconsistent with the situation. His expression wasn't fear, resignation, or even surprise. It was more like resolve when a shot came from his left, and the dark shape went down as Chase dove for cover.

As he rolled to get back up, the dark shape rose also and quickly fired twice toward whoever had shot him. Looking over his shoulder, Chase saw Caruso get hit and go down as he turned and took full advantage of the lull, shooting the dark shape three times. From this distance and limited light, all appeared to have been Alpha or Charlie hits, meaning head and upper chest.

Chase spun toward Caruso. "Caruso, you, okay?" There was no answer. With his gun still out, he walked slowly toward the man he had just shot. The dark shape of the large man was down, and even though the sunlight was fading, his wounds were dramatic.

He didn't know it then, but he had just killed Bernard Decco.

Chase turned and headed back to Caruso. He got down next to him, "Caruso, hang in there. I'm going for help." Caruso was still alive but said nothing, using his eyes to acknowledge Chase who then solemnly headed for Alycia.

It was dark now as he approached the body that lay on the grass face down next to the lake. It was actually a beautiful spot, and his eyes became a little moist at the thought, but he brushed it off and kneeled, checking for a pulse. Surprisingly, she had one, but it was slow. She had been shot in the back, though, to her upper chest. Not good.

With minor bleeding wounds to his hand, arm, and shoulder, it was going to be tough, but without hesitation, he hoisted her up into his arms. He gave a grunt of pain as he did so and used his legs to stand. Because of her chest wound, he couldn't put her over his shoulder as he had done so many times as a SEAL. But to him, Alycia had earned the right to be one of them, and he wasn't about to let her die on the battlefield.

As he stood with her in his arms, he turned to walk back to the cabin when her head rolled toward him, causing him to scream.

Chapter 42
Chase Residence, Kalispell

Jenkins stood with Stone as the dead were identified and the wounded were being prepared for transport. The highway in front of the house had been closed in both directions and was currently a sea of emergency vehicles when Jenkins asked Stone, "Have you seen Caruso?"

"No, not sure where he was last. What about Chase?"

"Last time I saw him, he was headed out toward the mountain. I think the young attorney panicked and was headed that way."

"Looks like that was a fatal error," Stone said as he pointed. "Here he comes now."

Chase was a few hundred yards away, walking toward them, his right side hanging down, his entire arm bloody as both men ran to help. As they approached, the man they saw looked nothing like Richard Chase. His gaunt face was etched in pain as Jenkins thought to understand the situation and said, "Richard, let us help."

But he shook his head no and, in a deep, almost exorcist voice, said, "Get a paramedic, Billy. Nobody else touches her," and he kept walking.

Jenkins had never seen his friend in so much pain, and as Stone went to help, Billy stopped him. "I'm not sure what's going on, but leave him be. Richard is doing this because he has to. I just don't know why."

Chase had passed them in a silent trance, and they, in turn, started to head back. Stone went to get a paramedic. Jenkins headed toward Richard when he saw Cheyenne and Alex walking on the road toward him. He said to himself, "Holly shit, what are they doing out here?" thinking they had been in the cabin.

Richard had taken the body up on the back patio just as two paramedics came running, and together, they laid her down on a table and went to work.

Both were treating her, but clearly, Richard also needed medical attention, although he had just stood there. Their frantic actions highlighted the seriousness of the situation.

Jenkins turned and headed to the girls. "Hey kids, where are you coming from? How did you get out of the cabin?"

As they approached, the full force of what had just happened with Richard hit Jenkins like a Mack truck. Alex was there in front of him, and Alycia was standing just behind her dressed like Cheyenne.

Oh Shit! Richard had been carrying Cheyenne, dressed like Alycia.

Chapter 43

Kalispell Regional Medical Center, Day Ten

Richard sat in the Critical Care waiting room alone in the corner, away from the television. There was a family in the opposite corner, and they were all as somber as him, their tears reflecting bad news as they tried to cope. Cheyenne had lost both her parents early in her life, but tribal elders had been there earlier in a show of support. Dr. Kingman had stopped by, as had Sheriff Jenkins. Special Agent Stone would have, but he had been sequestered by FBI command.

Somewhere in this same wing of the hospital, Special Agent in Charge Damion Caruso was being treated, but was not expected to survive. It bothered him that Caruso was being hailed as a hero, but that wasn't his fight, especially since Caruso likely saved his life when he shot Decco. But at that moment, other demons in Richard's head were taking over his thoughts.

The strange situation with Darna, his immense love for his son and the reality of his dangerous profession. Front and center were the painful thoughts of Cheyenne who was clinging to life. It didn't help that they had still not solved the case although the death of Decco and likely Caruso would slow the enemy down.

Late the night before, he had learned from Alex and Alycia about the clothes swap. He was furious at Cheyenne for doing it, let alone leaving the cabin, but at the same time, proud of her. She found a ploy to save the younger girls and bravely executed it. It was clear from where they were that if the FBI had not arrived, the cabin would have been compromised in some manner.

The door opened and an older doctor came out and walked toward him. All business, no smile. When he arrived in front of Richard, he stood and the doctor said, "Morning."

"Morning," Richard said.

"Your friend is resting in a medically induced coma, and she'll stay there for at least twenty-four hours to let her internal injuries heal. If her vitals stay where they are or improve, we'll start to bring her back."

"She was shot in the upper back."

"Yes, the bullet entered her back and came out within an inch of her lung and heart. It was fortunate for her vital organs, but the bullet did extensive damage. I would say that her surgery was as successful as it could have been."

"Will she make it?" he asked stoically.

"The next twenty-four hours are critical. She's in God's hands now, so pray for her. It is all any of us can do now."

The Chase property was still a crime scene, and more than a dozen CSIs, Sheriff, and FBI personnel were on site, cataloging the evidence from the previous day. The militants who entered Fortitude had made a hell of a mess trying to access computers as they searched for the documents, all of which were in the cabin. Chase had his field team remain since the Kalispell agent for Cartwright was still unknown, and Manny had just left to pick up Nate from the neighbors several miles away. Chase should have left him there for another day, but he needed to see his boy. He needed something to ground him.

Alex, Eddy, and Alycia could not enter the barn, so for now, the documents were spread out on the coffee table in the cabin. They each sat with a stack, going over each page, looking for any facts they did not already possess. Agent Stone had also given a copy to his command, so as the three of them sat there somewhere, the FBI resources were trying to locate the same facts.

The mood of the table was a mixture of tiredness, sorrow, and frustration. They all felt for Cheyenne, especially Alycia, but perhaps even more so because they had not uncovered the reason for all of this.

Eddy looked at the stack of completed papers and those left. "This really sucks. We're almost through the pages and have little to show for it. Alycia, what made you think these files were so different from the Cayman files."

"Primarily because the Cayman files come from each attorney. In the case of Enrique and me, we wrote them and put them there so I know what they contained. It might have been news to you, but not us. The archives at Cartwright, however, are said to be created by a committee. Nobody knows exactly who is on it, but it is rumored to include the Cartwright brothers, Decco, and the head of IT."

Eddy shrugged, "Okay, fine. But if these are handcrafted, then why doesn't it appear that they contain new information?"

"I just don't know," Alycia said, truly baffled. "Maybe these were decoy documents, and the real ones were on another server."

"No way. It was like breaking into Fort Knox to get to these," Eddy replied.

The team would spend another three hours before there were no longer two stacks. There was only one, meaning they had gone through all the pages. Dejected, they all went to the living room when the front door opened and Richard entered. He hung up his coat and sat down. "Hey."

"How is Cheyenne?" Alex asked, as if nothing else mattered.

His reply was said softly and without emotion. "She made it through surgery and is in a medically induced coma. The next twenty-four hours are critical. Is Nate home yet."

"Manny just left to get him."

"Okay," Chase stood and looked outside and noticed the FBI was still there. "Have they released the barn?"

"Not that we know of. That is why we're here."

"Okay. Somebody text me when Nate gets home." And he walked out and headed to the barn. After he spoke to one of the agents, they let him cross the tape and enter.

"So, are Richard and Cheyenne a couple?" Alycia asked.

Eddy turned red, but Alex replied, "Nobody knows. I say they have the hots for each other, but the boss is technically married to Nate's mom, who lives in the Philippines. She is so pretty."

"I know. I saw her picture. Why is she there instead of here?"

"No idea. Other than a few visits, she has never lived here."

"That's weird, right?"

"Totally, but the boss is a really private guy. It's hard to read him."

"I think he's handsome," Alycia said.

Eddy snapped, "Jeez, come on. I'm right here."

"Fine, sorry. So, what now?"

Eddy asked, "Alycia, we ignored the contracts because you said they were the same. Are you sure?"

"They weren't an addendum; they were the original contracts, so my reasoning was that they were the same as the Caymans."

"I didn't think about it until just now, but I'm not sure if they are. It took five banker boxes to hold the Cayman files, but only four to hold the archived files from Miami," Eddy replied.

"Are you saying they're smaller?" Alycia asked with hope.

"They have to be."

"They're in Richard's room. I'll go get one I wrote to compare."

She went down the hall to his room and opened the boxes until she came to one of her contracts and pulled it out. As she walked back, the picture of Richard's wife, Darna, was no longer there.

Just as she sat down, Nate entered, with Manny right behind him.

"Hi, Nate," Alex said, and the others waved.

Nate smiled and said, "Hey, everyone, where's Dad?"

"He's over in the barn and wanted to know when you got home."

Nate turned to Manny, "Can I go see him?"

"Sure, let me walk you over."

As they left, Alycia said, "That boy is going to be a freaking model when he's older. What a cute kid."

"What do you expect from his parents? Okay, where do we start?"

"Let me run through this quickly to see if the structure is the same," Alycia said as she flipped through each page.

At the entrance to Fortitude, Manny confronted the same agent, and he allowed Nate to go up and see his dad as long as he stayed in his office. Nate ran inside as Manny retreated towards the cabin.

Chase was in his office when he heard the unmistakable footsteps of his son before he saw him and smiled for the first time in two days. Nate ran to give his dad a hug when he stopped and frowned.

"Jeez, Dad, what happened to you?" noting the many bandages on his hand, arm, and forehead.

"Run in with some bad guys," he said as he stood and gave the boy a powerful hug.

"Is that why there's police everywhere?"

"Yep."

"And why I had to stay at the Pattersons?"

"Yep."

"And I suppose this is something I shouldn't tell mom."

"Well, I wouldn't, but you can if you think it's best."

"I saw the gang over at the cabin, but I didn't see Cheyenne. Is she here?"

Richard grew more serious and put his hand on Nate's shoulder. "Hey buddy, Cheyenne got hurt, too."

"What do you mean?"

"She's in the hospital, and we need to pray for her okay."

Richard wasn't raised in a religious house and had almost no exposure to organized religion growing up. But as he got older, he was quite interested in the history of religion. Many of his SEAL brothers were from different faiths, and their beliefs and rituals fascinated him. When someone asked about his faith, he would say he was spiritual, but not a churchgoer. As such, Nate had limited knowledge of praying in general, but he must have picked it up somewhere.

He jumped up, went to the window, got down on his knees, and placed his palms together in front of him, pointing towards the mountains behind the property. Richard smiled as his son closed his eyes and asked God to help Cheyenne.

Chapter 44

Cartwright & Cartwright, Miami

William Cartwright sat at his white marble desk, reading an article about synthetic shares in the options market. The concept was fascinating, and a professor was modeling how it could work. Suddenly, his intercom went off, "Mr. Cartwright, your brother is here and says it's urgent."

"Send him in." William smiled as he set the paper down and watched as his red-faced brother bounded toward him.

"Randle, you look ready to explode. Let's have a drink and calm you down."

They walked to a small sitting area, and while his brother poured drinks, Randle tried to slow his breathing. William handed him a tumbler, and both swished the brown liquid around the ice to cool it down. Randle thought Jameson's Irish Whiskey was woefully inadequate, but over ice, it was tolerable.

"What happened?" William said, more seriously now.

"It's about some Phoenix transactions."

"I'm listening."

"The death of Winston Bartholomew brought an inquiry from the FBI and a private security company in Kalispell, Montana. As you know, we had assistance stalling the FBI, but the security company has a relationship with hackers who uncovered more than they should."

"Uncovered what, Randle?"

"They hacked our archives and took our attorney. I believe it was the Gomes girl."

"When?"

"Three days ago, and I would have spoken to you, but you were traveling, and I needed time to create a defense."

"Which Mr. Decco has no doubt done," William said, as he smiled. When Randle didn't reply, he asked again. "Which Bernard has accomplished, correct?"

"Bernard Decco is dead, as is our FBI insider."

"And our files and attorney?"

"Still in Kalispel surrounded by the FBI and the local Sheriff's department."

"Can they possibly understand what they have?"

Randle hesitated but said, "Given the track record established over the last week, most certainly."

William was blunt. "Well, we had a good run, but the day we have always feared is upon us. Begin the sequence and leave for the Maldives tomorrow if possible. We'll meet there."

Randle nodded. The "sequence" was a method of pulling all the cash from the firm. And the Maldives were the location of their elaborate new life where no extradition treaty to the United States existed. The plan had been in place for many years.

Chapter 45

Fortitude Security, Kalispell

Richard was still in the barn when Alex, Eddy, and Alycia entered and went up to his office. He was trying to stay busy reviewing invoices when they walked in, and he could tell something had happened.

"What's up?"

Alex said in haste, "Alycia may have found it."

Chase said nothing, but looked at Alycia.

"So, we found nothing in the separate pages. That made us go back to the contracts because Eddy noticed the archived versions were smaller than the Cayman versions."

"Okay, what does that mean?"

"I reviewed all six Phoenix files that Enrique and I created. In the Cayman contracts, they list specific investments. They vary from strip malls to condo projects."

"I follow you so far. We found them as well."

"In the Cartwright archives, the same contract is there, except the pages that detail the investment are not. Instead, the investment is part of an asset fund. In short, they are pooling the investors' cash to make a single, enormous investment. When the company is purchased, or the building is built, you get back your money with a fifteen percent return. It made perfect sense until we investigated the investments themselves." She looked at Eddy.

"None exist, boss. I mean, not even one."

"So, where did the money go?" Richard replied.

Alycia answered. "It went to Trinity. The participants of the Phoenix files are unwillingly taking part in a giant pyramid scheme. Each new investor is paying the interest to the old investors who, more often than not, let the principal ride. As long as they earn their fifteen percent, none are aware that there are no assets behind their money or that their money is really gone."

Dumbfounded, Richard said, "Shit. I need to get Jenkins and Stone involved. Alycia, write up a summary that I can give to the FBI. Meanwhile, you all hang tight here, and do not leave. Stay away from the windows as well. We still don't know the identity of the local person from Cartwright, but my guys will make sure you're safe."

It was an hour later when Chase arrived at the Sheriff's station where Jenkins and Stone had already gathered. Jenkins had been explaining how his command had received the story Stone had created and there were no issues as far as he knew.

Stone had it a bit worse. While the FBI command was pleased with the outcome, they frowned at the lengths to which Caruso and Stone had gone without proper approvals. It would have been worse, but Caruso had died earlier in the afternoon, and out of respect, the inquiry was muted. All morning, Stone was grilled on the many facets of the investigation, and while he likely screwed up somewhere, it would be a while before they linked any inconsistencies.

Looking at the others, Stone said, "So basically, the traitor is the hero, and I'll take a few hits for the protocol violations, but it won't be long-lasting. We'll have to understand this whole thing soon, however. As of this minute, the big guns are on their way in, and when they get here, we'll be officially out."

Chase smiled. "I think I can help with that. Alycia and my kids figured it out," as he told them about the pyramid scheme.

"Holly shit, Bart was duped?" Jenkins said, amazed.

"I think so, but let's pay a visit to Katherine. If I'm right, she had nothing to do with his death," Chase replied.

Sheriff Jenkins's truck came into the cul-de-sac and drove to the gates in front of Bartholomew's house. His light bar was off, and he keyed in the code to activate the gates and thankfully the reporters had left for bigger stories.

Driving up to the circular driveway, he stopped at the front, and all three piled out while Billy did the honor of ringing the bell. Katherine opened the door and saw the three men. Her expression clearly showed she wasn't happy with the visit.

"Morning Katherine, we need to talk."

"And it takes three forms of law enforcement to do so?"

"We think we got this all figured out, but we need your help."

"I'm told you're all out and FBI is sending in a proper team." Still not opening the door for them.

Not in the mood, Billy stopped her. "Katherine, we have spent endless hours on Bart's death, and last night, we almost died for your cause. The only reason a new team is arriving is because the nature of the case has changed. Thanks to our efforts."

Katherine stiffened. "Am I in trouble, Sheriff?" she said, clearly thinking that was the case.

Jenkins looked around at the others and replied, "No, ma'am."

On that, Katherine stood back and allowed them in and led them to the living room where they all sat.

Jenkins took the lead. "Here is what I believe, Katherine. Winston learned about your brother Matthew's connection with Trinity and Cartwright. He meets with you, and together, you decide to invest to see how the transaction works. Is that close?"

She held herself for a moment, but her hands were trembling and after a brief silence, she nodded her head.

"It was Larry who discovered Matthew was with Trinity Holdings and told me. I was concerned and told Bart because he knew Trinity was a subsidiary of Cartwright from the hearing. And yes, we made the investments through Matthew. Part was so he would earn a commission to get funds he desperately needed, and the other was to understand what they were up to. We earned fifteen percent on the first three transactions but have not yet earned anything on the others. The money was left in the fund."

Stone asked. "Mrs. Bartholomew, the local investments we mentioned, were those the assets you thought you were buying?"

"As I told you, the investments you mentioned were not what we invested in, and I had never heard of them before. What we invested in were foreign infrastructure funds. Nothing is related to those local investments."

"They're all fake," Chase added as Katherine looked worried.

Jenkins continued. "We further think that certain people within Cartwright made the connection between your brother and Bart. It took a while since our blood evidence was taken. Eventually, we discovered an email from Cheyenne to Dr. Kingman that contained a picture of the electrograph of the killer's blood. It was a match for Matthew, and during the autopsy, a minor bullet wound was found on his side, where we believe Bart shot him. We believe Cartwright threatened Matthew and forced him to kill Bart. He did so thinking it would save him, but they then killed him spectacularly once he returned to New York."

Saddened, Katherine began to tear up and said softly, "Then I'm glad they did. So, what happens now?"

"I cannot comment on that, but the Cartwright empire will suffer a deadly blow in the next forty-eight hours."

"Will I lose my money?"

"We believe you already have, although the assets of the Cartwright brothers may offer some restitution. I'm sorry."

As she began to cry, they all glanced at one another, thinking she was upset about the money when she said, "We should have let it go. Bart knew what kind of people they were, but I insisted. I wanted to punish them and punish my brother. Oh God, look what I've done."

Jenkins handed her a tissue. "Katherine, Bart, died doing what he always did, trying to understand something crooked and save others. We'll make sure the press shows him in the proper light."

"Can I ask if Mark and Angie Griffin are involved in all this?"

"All will be revealed in a few days, but for now, stay away from them."

"So that is a yes."

"Just stay away from them both until we know for sure."

Katherine just nodded, and they let themselves out.

As they left, A woman looked out of the office window at the Midwest location of Griffin Enterprises. She let go of the curtain and went to make a cup of tea. As she passed Griffin's office where he was still working, she asked if he wished for a cup as well.

Returning to Fortitude, Alycia had typed up a synopsis, which Alex sent to Chase, Stone, and Jenkins. Stone sent it right away to headquarters in the J. Edgar Hoover Building in Washington. If they read it, it would point the analysts to the pyramid scheme, and by morning, the machine would be in motion to raid Cartwright & Cartwright.

Chapter 46

Kalispell Regional Medical Center, Day Eleven

It had taken much of the day to assist Stone with the details and evidence they had acquired. The reason was to create the base case for the new Special Agent in Charge arriving from Washington in the afternoon. Despite the upcoming change, Jenkins and Chase felt good about the work they had done. They further hoped the FBI would hunt this all down quickly, using the stage they had set.

A second objective was to facilitate a raid on the Midwest location of Griffin Enterprises. Stone had received a warrant, and they were planning to raid the Griffin home in advance of the arrival of the new agent. They were not concerned that he or she would disagree. Rather, they knew the local insider to Cartwright was monitoring the events of the recent shoot-out and the change in tactics. Under that line of thinking, they feared whoever it was would escape and acknowledged that she may have already done so.

Chase would not be involved in the Griffin raid and the FBI would not allow it, anyway. So, after leaving the agency, he stopped at the hospital just a mile away to check on Cheyenne. He had assumed they would call him if something changed, but if they were busy or knew he wasn't immediate family, it might not register how important it was. At least to him.

Heading to the fifth floor, he entered the CCU wing and approached the nurse's station. There, he asked if it was possible to visit her, but the request was denied, and he reluctantly went into the waiting room.

As he entered, he thought what a strange place this was. It was a place one hated but liked at the same time. Inside that room, you were going to get good news or bad news. Be elated or devastated. Hopeful or distraught, but you had to be there to get either emotion. He chuckled to himself, Richard "Rottweiler" Chase, a philosopher.

Sitting down, he recalled Nate giving Cheyenne a prayer in his highly animated way, and now, silently, Richard did as well. Considering his most recent thoughts, he was surprised when the doctor came into the room not fifteen minutes later. But instead of heading to him, he walked to a small family who were all in some form of distress and once he spoke, Chase knew that face, that expression. The one that likely included the words, "We did everything we could."

Suddenly, he didn't want to be there and stood to leave. Maybe he wanted to avoid bad news. He had made it a few feet toward the door when the voice of the doctor bellowed over his shoulder. "Mr. Chase?"

He turned, and the doctor walked toward him. "Sorry, it has been a tough morning. I can take you back."

"Back where?" Richard said, unsure why the doctor would apologize to him.

"Oh, I'm sorry," he said surprised. "I just assumed you wanted to see Ms. Denton."

"I do, but the nurse said I wasn't allowed."

"Usually, patients on this floor can only be seen by direct family, but I'm not aware that Ms. Denton has family. And besides, you're the only one who has held a vigil here. You also look like you would use some good news."

Richard laughed, "Are you saying there is good news?"

"Come on, young man, follow me."

Richard followed the doctor and was taken to a single room, CCU 512. It was an inside room with no windows and was relatively dark, with mood lighting coming from beneath the hospital bed. He imagined this was for the nurses and not the patients' benefit. The doctor pointed inside, saying, "Try to limit your stay to thirty minutes."

"Thank you," Richard said, not at all sure what was happening but that there must be good news associated with it. He entered the room, and Cheyenne was on her side, sleeping between pillows, making sure she could not turn to her back or stomach. This poor girl.

He pulled up a chair and just watched her. She seemed peaceful, her breathing normal, and although her pulse seemed very low, all the monitors suggested calm, which made him feel calm. He looked to the ground and said a silent thank you when Cheyenne, her eyes still closed, spoke in a soft, raspy voice.

"I hope you got them."

Richard stood immediately on hearing her weak voice and was emotional but trying not to show it. He walked over to face her. "We held our own and once the FBI came, it was over."

Opening her eyes, she looked at him. "You look like you've been in a catfight?"

"Yeah, something like that."

"Other guys are worse off, right?"

"Hell yeah."

"Are you mad at me?"

"Very, but I understand why you did it."

"Dr. Kingman must be angry as well. We were understaffed as it was."

"I'm happy to say he'll be elated once he finds out you're okay. I always thought he was such as ass, but he's fond of you and very concerned."

"Thanks," as her eyes closed. "It's funny. I haven't been in a hospital for sixteen years, and now, twice in the same week. Both times with a gunshot wound, and both times, I woke up to see you."

"What can I say? I'm a good luck charm."

"Big teddy bear is what you are."

He laughed. "Not really, I just wanted to sneak a peek at your wolf tattoo," he said as a joke, although on some level, it was true.

She tried to laugh and immediately caught herself. That was not fun, and she winced at the sudden pain in her chest. It took a second to subside.

"My wolf's spirit saved me, and I would love to show it to you once I no longer have a hole in my left breast," she replied.

"Good to know," as they both smiled.

Chapter 47

Cartwright & Cartwright, Miami, Day Twelve

The raid on Cartwright & Cartwright had been well planned. Seven SUVs had shown up unannounced, and over twenty FBI agents arrived at each of the four floors that the law firm controlled. Building security was brought in to block the stairwells and elevators. Simultaneously, on the heliport atop the Miami Tower, an FBI helicopter landed to block all potential escape routes and to drop off four more agents. It had taken just sixteen minutes to shut the company down, although questioning of the employees and forensic accounting work would take months.

Special Agent Max Harper arrived at the C-Suite with three others and headed straight for the office of William Cartwright. There he flashed his credentials to his executive assistant, but didn't wait for a reply and barged into the office. She came in behind him and said that Mr. Cartwright had left for the airport. He told an agent to stay with her and headed next door to Randle Cartwright's office. Although his assistant tried to stop them, he barged in as the shocked executive turned and contemplated his options.

"Randle Cartwright, I am Special Agent Max Harper, and you are under arrest. I assure you there is no place to go."

Cartwright was viewing his options, but knew he was just an hour too late. He said nothing as an agent approached him and, after being handcuffed, was taken to the elevator.

Harper, meanwhile, rushed back to William's assistant and got the information regarding the fixed base operator terminal from which William Cartwright was taking off. He headed to the elevators, but he didn't go down. Instead, he went up.

As he ran out to the helicopter, its rotors were still in standby mode on the heliport, as he circled his hand to say they were leaving. He barely had buckled in when it took off for the Miami International Airport. Their destination was the Signature Flight Services FBO terminal off Highway 948. Within minutes, he had also ordered a ground stop for the taxiway attached to the private jet service.

The plane, a Gulfstream G-Five, had just pulled back as the pilots completed their flight check sequence. The co-pilot had just requested clearance to approach the taxiway when the tower informed them of the ground stop. The lone passenger, William Cartwright, had been insistent on them leaving immediately.

As the sound of the turbines idled down, the impatient executive came forward and yelled, "Why are we still on the tarmac? Did I not make it clear I am in a hurry?" They had flown him before and he was the client you most wished to avoid. The guy was a real piece of work.

"You did, sir, but the tower has not given us clearance to taxi, and they report a ground stop. I'm sure it will be cleared up shortly."

"Ground stop. Bullshit, there are planes coming and going all around us."

The pilot noticed a flurry of emergency vehicles on the apron around the enormous airport. He wasn't sure, but they seemed to be headed this way, although it was unclear why.

Cartwright yelled, "Go damn it, we don't have time, go! Once we're on the runway, they can't stop us, and I'll sort it out later."

"Sir, I cannot go until I receive clearance."

"I don't care, go."

The pilot looked at the co-pilot and was about to turn off the engines when a helicopter appeared. It was flying just fifty feet off the tarmac and heading straight for them.

"What is this guy doing?" the one pilot said to the other, referring to the helicopter as the red lights of the ground vehicles came closer.

"No idea. I'm shutting down," the pilot yelled as Cartwright reappeared behind them.

"They're after me. I said go, and I meant go."

"Now listen ..." as the pilot turned to face the older executive who was now holding a gun aimed at him. The pilot turned and gave the aircraft some boost as it started onto the taxiway as he thought of ways to stall for time.

Suddenly, their communication system blurted, "CC777, this is the tower. There is a ground stop in effect for taxiway K. Stop your aircraft immediately."

The pilot continued to move the Gulfstream forward although under ten miles per hour, heading on taxiway K for ramp K1.

The tower boomed again. "CC777, this is the tower. You are in violation of a ground-stop order. Stop your aircraft immediately." The next conversation on the open channel was more ominous.

"All available security, General aviation aircraft CC777 is on closed taxiway K heading toward ramp K1 and runway 8L."

In front of them, the helicopter had slowed down and was just a hundred yards away when it stopped, hovered, and then turned sideways to reveal the FBI logo. The side door was open as Agent Harper aimed a high-powered rifle at the plane. Behind them, several vehicles had blocked the taxiway, and at least six others were closing in around the plane.

"Fuck this," the pilot said as he braked heavily and quickly began to shut down the engines.

"Go, damn it!" Cartwright yelled at the pilot, enraged. Seconds later, the co-pilot sprung from his seat and tackled Cartwright, knocking the gun out of his hand before giving him a few solid hits for good measure.

The Cartwright brothers, no doubt, had access to the best legal teams in the world, and they were going to need it.

But for now, they were both in custody.

Chapter 48

Griffin Residence, Bigfork

Sheriff Jenkins and his deputies had shut down the road that led to the cul-de-sac where the Griffin home sat. Three FBI SUVs drove down the sparsely populated road and onto the Griffin estate. Two vehicles headed for the perimeter. One drove onto the grass to stop just outside the employee entrance to the Griffin Enterprises wing of the house. The second was at the property's rear and within seconds, eight high-powered weapons were trained on the exits of the household.

The third SUV containing Special Agent Stone and three others pulled up to the house and approached the door. Angie Griffin opened it until she saw Stone and three FBI agents in black tactical armor, all with weapons. Her eyes were the size of quarters as she jumped back and tried to close the door. Stone pushed the door so hard she flew backward onto the floor. He showed her the warrant, and one of the agents placed her under arrest, tying her hands together with a wire tie. One agent stayed with her as the others ran down the hallway to the doorway that led to the office area. Angie Griffin had yet to utter a single word and looked in absolute shock and horror. Agent Stone wasn't sure why.

As they approached the office door, Stone forced it open and yelled, "FBI do not move. Mr. Griffin, reveal yourself." As he yelled, a half-dozen people turned, most of them screaming.

Griffin came out of the office and approached Jenkins, "What the hell are you doing?"

"Mark Griffin, you are under arrest," he said as he held up the warrant.

"Agent Stone, it is not what you think. Okay, I made a few investments through Cartwright & Cartwright, but those were legitimate investments made from personal funds. It has nothing to do with ..."

"Mr. Griffin," A woman said from behind him.

Griffin barked, "Not now, Claudine."

Ignoring him, she continued. "With all due respect, it is best if you say nothing. Allow the FBI to consider their error, and we can return to our work soon."

"Ms. Bouchard?" Stone asked Claudine.

She smiled at knowing he had figured out her last name. How clever he must think he is.

"Yes, Agent Stone."

"Which desk might yours be?"

It was barely perceptible, but suddenly, it hit Stone. The insider wasn't Angie Griffin but rather Claudine Bouchard.

She had said nothing as he handed Jenkins' device to one of his agents. "Find the phone."

"Ms. Bouchard, you are also under arrest as an accessory to the fact in the murder of Winston Bartholomew."

Griffin yelled, "Wait a minute, Stone, you are way off base here."

"Mr. Griffin, you have your own worries. Agent, please cuff Ms. Bouchard and escort her to transport. She'll be going to Washington while Mr. and Mrs. Griffin can be taken downtown."

"You are making a big mistake, Agent Stone," Bouchard said coldly.

"I have a news flash for you. We have raided Cartwright & Cartwright and have brothers William and Randle in custody. I'll do my best to get you adjoining rooms, but I can't guarantee that," Stone said with a smile.

Chapter 49

Chase Residence, Kalispell

The weather in Kalispell was improving. The flurries were gone, and the ambient temperature had risen to the mid-twenties. The fire was hot now, as Chase had put on a few extra logs.

His Ariat boots were on the hearth, and he opened his Pendleton jacket to cool down, moving his chair back some as he did. Nate was playing with the fire as he grabbed his orange soda and took a big swig. Chase smiled and instinctively grabbed his beer and did the same.

The soft glow of headlights came around the drive and stopped as the unmistakable sound of Jenkins Subaru Outback went quiet. Somewhere, a door opened, and soon, Billy Jenkins walked out with a glass of bourbon.

"Hey, Nate." He said as he walked over and pulled up a chair.

"Hi, Billy. Catch any bad guys today?"

"No, but I chased a few off," he said as he turned to Chase. "You need to restock the good stuff, Richard. I'm getting tired of making this drive for this supermarket crap."

"I'll get right on that. So, how was your day, dear?" Chase asked, and they both chuckled.

"About as boring as yesterday. Fortitude needs a new case to bring some action back to this town."

"You hear from Stone?"

"Yeah, he called yesterday. They offered him a SAIC position in Billings, but he turned it down."

"He prefers warmth, I suspect."

"Yes, but I think he likes the action. Did Alycia join the team?"

Billy was referring to an offer Chase had made to bring the attorney on at Fortitude as an analyst and legal advisor.

"No, she returned to Miami, closed out her lease, and according to Alex, she's moving back home with her folks. She was never charged, but the stigma of working at Cartwright has hurt her attempts to gain employment. Alex will stay in touch with her, and we still might be able to hire her if she can't find work. I probably couldn't afford her, anyway."

"I spoke to Katherine."

"How is she? I saw the house was for sale."

"It is, and she has already left for New York. Turns out she's more of a city girl. Did she thank you for our efforts?"

"She did and paid the tab for the Fortitude contract in full. Even gave us a nice bonus."

"She was kind to me as well. It made me feel guilty for suspecting her right to the end."

"Yes, but the assistant, Claudine? Never saw that coming."

"Stone says she's singing for a plea deal with the DOJ. What they have thus far is that Decco recruited her over a year ago once Bart's identity was known. The FBI is convinced she was organizing the actions out here, including Bart's murder, and it appears Mark Griffin had no idea of her true identity. The brothers are saying nothing, but forensic accountants have unearthed close to a billion dollar fraud with several hundred plaintiffs."

"Did they ever figure out how Bartholomew could have invested in the first place?"

"It was more or less what we discussed out here a few nights ago. Matthew needed the commission, so he created a fake account trying to hide Bart's identity. Apparently, nobody cared at first because the investment money was real, but when the first fifteen percent payment was made, they realized something was wrong. Pullman had apparently made the payment to himself to hide Bartholomew's address. Eventually, Decco roughed him up to find out

Bart and his wife were involved. He and Claudine created the plan to force Matthew into killing Bart, but only Decco knew Pullman would share the same fate."

Richard nodded.

Jenkins took a sip of bourbon and asked Richard, "Did we ever find out who the principal partners were in Trinity?"

"Actually, yes. Alex figured it out with one of her cipher programs. I guess I didn't mention it because it no longer mattered. If you take the first letter of the first and last name of each, Iyla Anderson, Alan McDonald, and Logan Ellis, you get six letters, IAAMLE. That means nothing, but those same six letters also spell Amelia. Apparently, the Cartwright brothers had a baby sister who drowned when she was just three. William and Randle used the deceased real persons to stand in for her name, and Amelia Cartwright is the true legal owner of Trinity Holdings."

"Of course. And the exclusive money managers for Amelia Cartwright are William and Randle?"

"You got it! What of Mark and Angie Griffin?" Richard asked.

"Ms. Griffin was released and knows nothing. Stone is still working Mark Griffin over for lying to a federal agent, but since Katherine did the same, which they are not pursuing, I doubt it will stick. It is worth knowing; he lost all his money, too."

"I'm sure he'll be fine," Chase said as Jenkins rose to refill as he walked into the house.

Nate set down the stick he was using to even out the coals. "Dad, is Cheyenne coming over?"

"Yep. She'll be here in a little while."

"Cool, I found another arrowhead and wanted to show it to her."

"Do you like Cheyenne?" Richard asked.

"You bet."

"I'm glad because I like her too. She might even stay over sometimes."

"Like a sleepover? Holly cow, how great is that? Can she stay tonight?"

"Not sure, but maybe. I haven't asked her yet, so this is between us, okay," He smiled, knowing he would have to tell Nate at some point what he was really thinking.

If you enjoyed this second installment of the Richard Chase Adventure series, please take a quick moment to provide a rating and review on Amazon. It is much appreciated. Stay tuned for the next adventure. Thanks.

Trust Me

Richard Chase's first reaction to his next adventure was that this case sounded like something from a Hollywood movie script.

An accountant in upstate New York dreams of finally making it big when he joins a small start-up company. But long before a share of stock is sold, he is arrested for embezzling millions from the company. Soon, he is in prison, with all evidence pointing to him, although the money is nowhere to be found.

Not surprisingly, he insists he didn't do it and is being framed. Chase initially wants no part of this but eventually commits himself and Fortitude Security to exonerate him for only one reason. The accountant is practically family.

Other Adventures

Richard Chase Adventures

Payback *(Book 1)*

Eye for an Eye *(Book 2)*

Trust Me*, (Coming 2025)*

Sara Ricci Scientific Thrillers

Deadly Dissertation *(Book 1)*

Deadly by Design *(Book 2)*

Deadly Discovery *(Book 3)*

Deadly Dilemma *(Book 4)*

Deadly Diplomacy *(Book 5)*

Deadly Distractions *(Book 6)*

Deadly Decisions *(Book 7, Coming 2025)*

Made in the USA
Columbia, SC
09 June 2025

71ca614c-d607-46d9-a76a-5fc5e97d388cR01